Coyote Still Going: Native American Legends and Contemporary Stories

Ty Nolan

Published by Coyote Cooks Press, 2014.

Coyote Still Going:
(Native American Legends and Contemporary Stories)
Ty Nolan
Copyright 2013 Ty Nolan

This is a work of fiction. Similarities to real people, places, or events are entirely coincidental.

COYOTE STILL GOING: NATIVE AMERICAN LEGENDS AND CONTEMPORARY STORIES

First edition. March 21, 2014.

Copyright © 2014 Ty Nolan.

Written by Ty Nolan.

10 9 8 7 6 5 4 3 2 1

To all my extended family who have shared so much with me. To the Tohets, Mitchells, Millers, and Bernals who taught me so much. And to the memory of my mentors--Carolyn Attneave and Bea Medicine.

Some voices have been silenced, but the Stories remain.

Coyote Still Going

Foreword

Here are some stories. For many years I have told these and other stories across the United States and many other countries. Often people "only" wanted me as a Storyteller. I was expected to tell stories for a specific amount of time and either leave the stage, or wait for an arriving audience so I could start the next performance. I served as an Artist-In-Residence as a Storyteller for school districts throughout California and Washington State. A DVD of my performance of *Coyote's Eyes* accompanied the 11th Grade edition of Houghton-Mifflin's *The Language of Literature* textbook, which gave me a national audience. I would often be recognized in airports by young people who would come up and tell me they had seen the DVD of me in their classroom.

On a personal level, I've spent much more time using variations of these stories when I was involved providing therapy for people seeking a change in their lives, or when I would keynote an educational or mental health conference. My standard procedure was to open up with a relevant traditional Story, and then spend the rest of my presentation developing the theme of the Story in the context of my audience's needs. I remember being told by the Medical Director of the clinic where I worked, "You will be best remembered for writing a book of *Coyote Stories for Sex Therapists*."

I formally began using legends in classrooms when I was Area Director for Head Start Programs on American Indian Reservations in five states. I was frustrated by the fact the classrooms had nearly 100% Native children, but there was absolutely nothing in the classroom that reflected the reality of these children, other than the fact the teaching assistants were also from the reservation, even though the actual head teacher or the Head Start Director, was almost always non-Native. The environment of those classrooms was not really different than a Head Start classroom in Kansas or Alabama. I would walk by a few Walt Disney Characters on the wall. A giraffe or an elephant would decorate the place. These were all standard preschool items dutifully ordered from a catalog.

I began demonstrating using some of the stories in this book to work with the children to teach them what the assigned learning objectives were. I would then ask the local Native people to help me do the same sort of things with their own legends, songs, and traditional items. For example, if children are learning to count, showing them a picture with five of the traditional baskets made in their community to illustrate the concept of "five" can be more effective than showing them a picture of five elephants. When they leave the classroom and see the same sort of baskets in their community, they will more likely remember the lesson, given the fact they would rarely see elephants outside of the classroom.

When I was asked to start keynoting early childhood development conferences, or bilingual education conferences to discuss my approach, I was frustrated because I would be surrounded by teachers and administrators who would come up to me afterward and ask if I could come to their community and tell their kids stories. My self-identity in that context was as a teacher-trainer/curriculum developer. But I was perceived as a performer the children would enjoy. I established a compromise. I would agree to come in and do a school assembly, for example, telling a series of stories. But I would also require teachers to attend an after-school training session where I would discuss the elements of storytelling, and why I had chosen the specific stories I had, and what responses I was seeking from my youthful audience.

Given my experience, I suspect some readers want to pick up a book that's labeled "Native American Legends" and expect to find a collection of American Indian Legends. Some readers will be parents or other family members who want to find something a little out of the ordinary to use as bedtime stories, and like the idea of exposing their children to a greater level of diversity than they might get from some standard European fairy tales. Others will pick up this book (or Kindle, Nook, Tablet, or whatever e-device is popular at the moment) because they are storytellers themselves and are always looking for something to add to their own performance repertoire. Some readers might be taking a class in anthropology or Native American Studies, and are hoping they won't only find a collection of American Indian Legends, but additional information that will provide a context for the stories and a deeper understanding of their meanings.

Some readers may be teachers or therapists who know very well how effective stories can be in working with others. Just so, I am challenged by how to share the stories. Instructional details or suggested therapeutic applications for specific stories may completely miss the expectations of someone who just wants the stories. My own image from having worked with countless children is—some want to be served a plate where none of the food touches the other food, and if you just want to eat the peas, you just eat the peas. Others want everything they can possibly squeeze out of a resource.

As a result—here is what I propose. I will offer a more detailed Forward and Introduction that sets up what this book is about and provides at least some level of cultural context for both the story itself as well as its performance. I will then provide a collection of written versions of a number of traditional Native American legends I have performed over the last four decades.

As I learned from my working with the lovely D.M. Dooling, who used to be the Editor of *Parabola: Myth and Quest for*

Meaning, and my friend, the delightful P.J. Travers, who blessed us with her stories of Mary Poppins, I will use the convention of "...as retold by," to indicate I am giving you something that may not be exactly what you would experience if you heard me tell the same story in person, or told by one of my relatives. I'm working within the constraints of the medium, either printed or electronic.

For example, when I'm doing a live performance, I'm usually using a hand drum, and the rhythm can influence the mood of an audience. In an actual presentation, repetition can increase the enjoyment of a story, as the Teller can change his or her pitch, tone, or loudness to give variety. The very act of walking towards (or away from) an audience will alter the sound. Simply reading the words on a page or display screen can't give the same experience. I have often seen non-Native performers deliberately leave certain parts of a traditional Native story out as "too repetitive" without understanding something is often repeated four times because it's part of the ceremony. Something is described or mentioned four times because it is reflecting the four cardinal directions, or the four seasons of the year, as you'll see later on with the Girl *Who Was Aiyaiyesh*.

This has even changed since I used to publish in *Parabola*. If you are reading this on an e-reader, the density of text is something I've learned to take into consideration. It's simply easier to read if I break the information into short paragraphs, rather than long ones.

I will also give examples of how I've used some of the stories when training mental health professionals in the area of substance abuse. I've used the same story in working with HIV/AIDS prevention. Another story was one provided to a non-Native storyteller who was looking for a short story to tell at the wedding of her friends. Another I'll use as an illustration of how it can be employed when teaching about Native American culture or spirituality.

I hope this approach will keep the "peas" from ever touching the "mashed potatoes" if that's a priority, while allowing readers who want additional levels of resources than a simple collection of legends told out of context. I trust the Stories. They will survive when I am long gone, just as they have survived when the voices of earlier Storytellers were silenced. The Song continues, even when you've forgotten who the singer had been.

But I'm also a product of my family. It was a great shock for me to take non-Native friends to visit my relatives on the various reservation communities within my extended family. My relatives would teach non-stop. They'd go into elaborate detail as to why we used this color rather than that color—what a particular gesture in a dance meant.

Long and long ago, our family used to dance for non-Native guests at the Tribal Resort, and I would usually be expected to also tell a legend. Before we would perform, our dad would pull us aside and tell us, "Remember, for some of these White People, this is the only opportunity they will ever have to meet real Indians. So you don't just get up and hop around. You tell them what your beadwork means. You tell them what it means when you hold up your eagle feather fan when the drummers hit the drum hard. You take every chance you get to teach them."

I didn't really understand that so much at the time. I just did what I was told. But now that I'm at least as old as he was when he was saying that, I suspect part of it represented a survival skill for a people the federal government had tried so hard to exterminate. It's the same thing we're seeing as state after state has legalized marriage-equality between same-sex couples. As humans, we can only successfully demonize people we have been taught to see as "other." When you are taught American Indian people are also human, or that members of the LGBT community are ultimately no different than another member of your family—it's hard to discriminate. Or as the Elders used to tell us—"When you point your finger at someone, three other fingers point back at you."

So—many years after audience members started asking me if I had written these stories down—I finally think I understand why I was not ready to do so at that time. Just as a physician doesn't give exactly the same medication to every patient with the same symptom (some patients would die of an extreme allergenic response), I used to hesitate simply handing over a version of a Story and then leaving. But I do trust in the Power of the Stories to take care of themselves. And to respect the memory of our dad—I also don't want to just "get up and hop around." I've been genetically programmed to teach.

Sadly, a few years ago I began to lose my vision from what I jokingly have called the "Trifecta" of eye diseases—glaucoma, cataracts, and low vision. I got to the point where I was no longer able to see the display screens in airports. I would usually show powerpoint images to illustrate the specific designs of baskets I refer to in my storytelling, and was at the point I couldn't see them clearly. I surrendered my driver's license, because I felt I had become a danger to myself and others. I started turning down requests for storytelling because travel had become so difficult for me.

I began to focus more on writing, since I could adjust my computer's display screen to at least 150% so I could read text more easily. I've now undergone six major eye surgeries (well, actually seven, but the first one was considered a failure) with the hope the deterioration of my vision has been slowed. However, the acceptance of my limitations encouraged me to go ahead and share some of these stories while I'm still able to do so.

So—here are some stories.

Introduction

Heeyaho—my name is Ty Nolan.

Here are some Stories as well as some stories. The title is a play on how many different American Indian/Native American Storytellers from different tribal nations will begin a Coyote traditional legend by saying—"Coyote was going there..." In Greg

Saris' *Keeping Slug Woman Alive*, he talks about his older relatives being interviewed by a non-Native scholar, who transcribed what they said in their Native language, but when she translated the stories into English, she used "Coyote was going there..." consistently.

Greg pointed out if you look at the actual transcripts the Elders used different verb forms, so in some cases Coyote was going there in a cocky manner. In other cases, Coyote might have been going there because he was frightened and running away. Maybe Coyote was going there because he was hungry—or knowing Coyote as I do, because he wanted to get jiggy. This is just the first example of how complicated translations can be, not only in terms of specific words (some of which have changed over the generations) but also because of the differences in terms of cultural concepts.

Coyote Still Going is an opportunity for me to share not only Native American Stories, but also to explore the traditional foods, personal stories and memories I have that blend in with the smell of Pueblo bread fresh from the outdoor oven—the crisp ashy taste of *pili* paper bread peeled from the stone griddle—or the cheesy white goodness of fresh salmon eggs after a few minutes under the broiler.

Over the years I've had the opportunity to travel many places in my work, and in the process, to experience wonderful people in Native communities and their foods and cultures across the United States and Canada. I've also been blessed with the chance to travel through Indonesia, Guam, Sai-Pan, and other places where indigenous cultures and their foods are still going strong.

Much of the material that appears in **Coyote Still Going** I prepared for a blog of mine I called **Coyote Cooks**. In the back of my mind, I had always wanted to explore the memories and experiences I've had related to our traditional foods, and the legends I had been taught as a Storyteller that frequently related back to how one feeds a community. In the Native homes I know, food (and water) is always considered to be sacred, and we were raised to never speak badly of food in its presence—because that animal or plant in essence gave up its life so your life could continue. If someone asks you if you like a food you find distasteful, you politely respond, "I respect this."

On Longhouse Feast Days, small bits of the traditional foods are placed on your plate. Then the bell ringer who is leading the prayer calls out the Native names of the specific foods, and you eat them. Finally, he or she calls out the Native word for "water," and you take a sip, because we were raised to understand taking a sip of water is always a type of prayer. This is something a lot of non-Natives don't understand when they see us take a sip of water before a meal. For us we begin with a prayer—but it's one of a physical movement, just as a worship dance is a prayer made visual.

An anthropologist friend shared her experience when she first started studying the culture of an Apache community. During their feasts, she would watch them as they took a pinch of salt from a bowl at the end of the table and sprinkle it over their food. She thought to herself "how unhygienic." Just so, she proudly went out and bought salt shakers, and carefully filled them, replacing the open bowl of salt with the shakers.

As she watched, the local people put their food on their plates, got to the end of the table and discovered the salt shakers. Each one put his or her plate down, picked up the shaker and shook out the salt onto an open palm. Then they took a pinch of the salt and sprinkled it over their food as they had always done.

And it was at that precise moment my friend understood the Apache people she was watching were making the sign of the Circle as a blessing on their food, much in the way some Christian groups will make the sign of the cross on their bodies as they are praying. Sometimes you can see, but that doesn't mean you always understand what it is you are seeing. And take this with a grain of salt, since it's coming from someone who is visually impaired.

I know some readers want to just go immediately to the traditional legends, so I've set up the Table of Contents to allow them to do just that.

And so—here are some Stories as well as some stories. And sometimes—if you pretend the recipes I've included will work, they actually will. I hope you enjoy this unusual and often tasty selection of more than one type of Oral Tradition as much as I have living them.

Chapter One

While I had learned many of the Stories I use when I was much younger, I didn't really start performing them publically until I became one of the Founding Members of the Red Earth Performing Arts company. One of our first performances was for Bumbershoot, a major annual festival event in Seattle. It was a great thrill to see our name on the marquee of the old Seattle Opera House.

At the time most of us were in our twenties, and we were very serious about wanting to do heavy duty drama, such as Hanay Geiohgama's moving play, **Body Indian**. Hanay explored the ravages of Native alcoholism in great detail. Let's just say it wasn't a musical. I played one of the teen characters. We received excellent reviews, but we tanked in terms of ticket sales. Not everyone wants to spend an evening watching some of the worst things about American Indian culture you can put on stage.

We were much more successful doing plays based on Native American legends. The first one was a kind of mish-mash of legends plucked from various Northwest cultures the non-Native playwright had discovered via the public library. I was cast as Shadowman, the villain of the play. Disappointment in the quality of the script inspired one of my relatives, Bruce Miller, usually called *Sobiyax* (his Twana Indian name) to write **The Changer**.

The Changer was based on Twana Creation stories. Many of them fit well into a theatrical format, hardly surprising for a culture with a strong tradition of storytelling that would almost always incorporate singing and dancing. A story/act would explain how Loon got his spots, or why Deer has cloven hooves. Initially we used our connections with the Pacific Science Center to borrow their authentic First Nations carved wooden dance masks. The Center had purchased an actual First Nations Longhouse from British Columbia, and reconstructed it within the Center's main building.

It was a major attraction for public schools, where teachers would bring their fourth grade students (the year primary school curriculum touches on Native American history) and the masks and related educational activities would be shared.

We were also gifted with the generosity of Bill Holm. At the time, Bill was Curator of the Burke Museum at the University of Washington. He is a well respected expert on Native culture, and has been adopted into a Kwakiutl family. He is the person who took the Edward Curtis silent film, ***In the Land of the Headhunters***, which had magnificent footage of Kwakiutl dances and regalia, and went back to their people and recorded a sound track to go with it.

Some of the elders had been children at the time of the filming, and remembered Curtis. They watched the silent footage and were able to match the songs the film had visually captured. For example, they would watch a canoe scene and know what paddle song to sing based on the rhythm they saw demonstrated on screen.

Bill told me after he had returned home to edit the final version—he realized he needed to add some excitement in a scene on the beach. Surrounded by non-Native technicians, he decided to teach them the Kwakiutl word for "hurry up." Unfortunately, the non-Natives weren't very fluent in Kwakiutl, and if you ever listen to the soundtrack, you will hear several people shouting "Weekends! Weekends!"

Bill was also a "hobbyist." If you're unfamiliar with this term, it refers to non-Native people who are interested in Native cultures and strive to accurately replicate traditional regalia and objects. Bill was also active at a period in time where he would be able to go to pawnshops near reservations and purchase traditional objects. He was meticulous at his attention to details and authenticity in recreating things.

One year I was asked to accompany my mentor, Carolyn Attneave, to the twenty-fifth anniversary celebration for the Mister Roger's television program. We were going to do a presentation and I wanted to tell the legend of Ant and Bear (which I'll include later as "Why Ant Has A Small Waist"). Unfortunately, I had met with a disaster in Anchorage. For ages I would attend American Indian/Alaskan Native conferences, and most would feature dances in the evening. I was envious of other attendees who had packed their regalia and proudly joined in.

I decided I would bring my own outfit for a conference in Alaska. I had a great time, and then someone broke into my rental car and stole my suitcase. I lost my beaded buckskin leggings, my entire outfit, including an eagle feather bustle and fan. My greatest loss was a woven cornhusk belt purse my grandmother had made when she was a young woman. I had been given it at her funeral—it could never be replaced.

Knowing I wouldn't have time to go home to pick up something else to wear before we flew off to Pennsylvania to celebrate Fred Rogers, I decided to ask Bill for help. He was kind enough to loan me an antique set of Crow beaded cloth leggings and loincloth. I had other items at my apartment—moccasins, belt, hair ornaments, etc., that hadn't been stolen in Anchorage.

I did my presentation, and an older White woman came up to compliment me. One of the realities a lot of Native people experience is having non-Natives do things to us they wouldn't think of doing to relative strangers. This includes touching or pulling on our braids, or grabbing on to our clothing. I have never felt this to be meant as disrespectful or mean-spirited, but a very child-like display of wonder. The woman looked down at my borrowed loincloth, and lifted it up to inspect it more closely.

The Crow man who originally wore the leggings was probably a bit shorter than I am. That meant there was a greater flash of my naked thighs when she lifted up the loincloth than I would have preferred. Let's just say I felt a significant breeze. In the story, Ant and Bear compete against each other—as in some non-Native stories, Ant is portrayed as very industrious and with a strong work ethic. Bear is more focused on eating than he is on the contest. The Ant wins. After the woman let go of my loincloth, she told me how much she enjoyed the story "...because I'm Bear."

Now I was puzzled. When I asked her why, she replied, "Because I'm fat and lazy and I eat a lot and Bear was not punished for being Bear." And she was absolutely right. As you'll find out later on when I share the full Story, the teaching isn't about winning a contest.

This is the other thing one learns as one ages—the Story may stay the same, but the audience changes. There are things I discover in a legend I have told for years because I have more experiences and points of references now than I did when I was a college freshman. When you start having parenting responsibilities, you begin to listen to Stories as a parent.

For Red Earth, Bill had loaned us an enormous wooden box drum. Most of my contribution was using this box drum to sing the songs for the play. I also would wear the carved wooden bear dance mask to portray how Bear became the first Medicine Person. My other major role was Crane.

How Bear Became the First Medicine Person

Long time ago, the Changer was changing everything—giving everything a purpose and a reason for being. He changed the course of rivers—made mountains—and gave the Animal People the shapes they wear today. At that time all the People were Animals, but they didn't look like they do today. They looked more like Human People. But in those days, reality was more flexible and they could shift back and forth into different forms.

When the Changer saw Bear, Bear was dancing upright, marking his territory by reaching up and clawing the trees around him. The Changer watched Bear carefully gathering plants to use. "Go forth and be Bear forever," the Changer told him. "You are the only one of the Animal People who will keep your original form. Human People who are to come will watch you and know the plants you gather can be used for medicine. You will be the first Medicine Person."

How Crane Became Crane

As the Changer continued on his way, he ran across Crane, who was using his hand for a hammer and his head for a wedge to split wood. This gave him a splitting headache. The Changer took pity on Crane and told him to go forth in the shape we see today. One of the teachings of Crane is how he will stand for a long time and then strike quickly to spear a fish. The Elders remind us that action should follow careful contemplation.

I think what I enjoyed the most from my Red Earth experience was watching the joy a lot of Native people had in being introduced for the first time to live theater—and to Native actors. The group had been started by John Kauffman, who at that time was a successful actor in Seattle, having graduated from the theater program at the University of Washington. He was approached by Bernie Whitebear, the Executive Director of the United Indians of All Tribes Foundation.

Bernie had a dream of an elaborate Native American complex that would include an art studio, shops, restaurant, a powwow dance arena, and a dinner-theater. He recruited John to make Red Earth a reality, with the expectation we would be heading up his dinner-theater. Unfortunately, there was a major backlash by members of the nearby wealthy White neighborhood who were named "NIMBYs" or "Not In My Back Yard!" They effectively killed Bernie's dream, or at least restricted it to a single building.

This was the Daybreak Star Cultural Arts Center. It was designed to symbolize the vision of Black Elk and the concept of the Four Directions that would indicate the eventual unity of all people in the Seventh Generation. I was part of the local community that volunteered to come in and scrape the bark off the large cedar logs that had been donated for its construction by the Quinault Nation. I served as one of the first Arts Directors for the Daybreak Star. A non-Native administrator walked by while I was busy making my button blanket to use with our Red Earth production, and he offered me the job on the spot. Luckily I had more qualifications than being able to sew on buttons.

We ended up receiving a bicentennial grant to tour seven western states. In addition to performing **The Changer**, we would also go into schools on various reservations and split into smaller groups to perform for individual classrooms. The kids were so excited, and just a delight as an audience. I remember being in South Dakota and as we were walking into the school, a little Lakota girl looked at my braids and ran into her classroom, "Teacher! Teacher! There's an Indian!" Her teacher looked at her and said, "What do you think you are?"

The experience of telling legends and performing on reservation schools eventually led me to serve as an Artist-In-Residence in school districts throughout Washington State and California. It was often grueling work to do eight class periods of Storytelling for weeks at a time. Many of the legends have specific dances and songs, so Storytelling can be a very physical activity. Depending on the age of the students and available physical space, whenever possible I would teach the students the relevant songs and dances, so they could perform them with me.

There are specific Stories that were intended for very young children to join in and perform. For twitchy children with a lot of energy (which is sort of the job description for many children) a legend I enjoy using is Why Rabbit Has Long Ears (provided I have the physical space to have the little ones move around. Fortunately, the dance can be modified so they can stay in one place.

Why Rabbit Has Long Ears

Long time ago, there were Rabbit children. Now you might think because of Peter Rabbit, and Bugs Bunny, and the Easter Bunny that these Rabbit children would be friendly and fun.

But you would be terribly wrong. These Rabbit children were mean! They didn't respect others. The never did what their Elders told them to do. They were probably the sort of children that never washed behind their ears.

One day they were out in the woods and they saw Mole Woman. They realized the old woman was almost blind and they thought of something very wicked to do because they knew she couldn't see who they were and tell their parents. Just so, they picked up sticks from the ground and started poking that poor lady!

"Help me!" she cried out. Suddenly there was a flash of lightning and the Creator stood before them. He was so angry at what they had done, he pulled them away from Mole Woman by grabbing their ears. As he yanked their ears, they stretched out and He said, "From this day forward, your Indian name will be Quwetchidy. (In English it means "stretched ears.") You will be rabbits!"

Now the in preparing the children, I ask them to stand up and point their index fingers. I explain these are their sticks and they are doing to pretend to "poke the old lady," in the rhythm of the song. When I sing, "Quwetchidy, Quwetchidy," they then put their index fingers up to their foreheads to show off their new ears, and when I'm singing "Rabbit, Rabbit," they are supposed to jump up and down.

This is one of the very many things I learned from an old friend, Ruthanna Boris, who was known as Balanchine's Ballerina, and toured with the Ballet Russe de Monte Carlo as the roommate of Maria Tallchief. When it comes to movement on a small stage she told me: "If you can't go out, then you go up."

We had met when she was Chair of the Dance Department at the University of Washington and volunteered to work with our clinic. She had also been trained to be a Freudian analyst. When she discovered I was a traditional American Indian dancer, she insisted I take her ballet classes. I ended up taking three years of ballet, and they were some of the toughest and most demanding courses I've survived. The best thing about not having to take any more ballet classes never having to wear a dance belt again.

One of the other personal things of value I took away from the classes was discovering I could take my soft soled moccasins to shoe repair shops that were used to working with ballet dancers, and I had the thicker leather soles used in ballet slippers sewn to the bottom of my moccasins. It made walking on city sidewalks a much more enjoyable experience, and I didn't have to spend a lot of my time sewing up holes that had worn their way onto my moccasins anymore.

Sometimes when I was in the schools and at the last class period, rather than sticking with my regular performance, I'd just have kids call out the names of different animals and I'd tell a legend about them. I thought it was a good idea to keep things fresh for me, but often the younger children would yell out "Kitty!" or "Cow," and I'd have to explain a lot of the animals they knew about weren't actually originally from the Americas, but had been imported by Europeans. However, even though we didn't have the domestic cat, I was able to tell the story about Lynx. Coyote was trapped in ice and Lynx used his rough tongue to scrape Coyote free. As a reward, Coyote pulled some of his own whiskers out and stuck them in Lynx's ears to make him look even more handsome.

I mentioned adapting traditional ideas into a contemporary environment. One of the activities I would do was to use "cue cards" I had created, instructing my youthful audience to play the musical instruments I had brought (drums, rattles, whistles, etc.) and teach them the legend's song. After telling the legend in the "standard" way, I'd ask them to help me retell it. I had a student read the legend I had written down, which freed me to hold up the cue cards and help with the singing.

For example, when Coyote was running towards the Mountain, I'd have them slap their palms on their thighs to create the "sound effect" of running. When he got to the Mountain, he was very tired and he began to pant, so up would go the cue card for "Pant!" When Coyote falls and hits the Mountain, all the students with drums would hit them hard, all at the same time. If we had the time and space, I'd also teach them a round dance to go with the Stars' song.

After one rehearsal, I'd turn on a tape recorder and we'd perform the legend. I would then play back the finished tape, which had become a radio style performance of the legend, along with "special sound effects" that I would then donate to their resource center. I also worked with the teachers to have the students illustrate the story, and the drawings would go with the tape, the way some contemporary stories have an audio form that goes with the matching "picture book." I wanted kids to get used to the idea they could produce curriculum. Many of the teachers would also mail me some of their students' creations.

Since I traveled so much, I would introduce students on reservations in say, Nevada, to those in Washington State, so they could exchange these Native creations with each other.

The particular one I used was a Sahaptin version one of my Aunts used to tell:

Coyote In Love With A Star

Long time ago, Coyote loved the night. As he watched the stars come out, he saw one was far more beautiful than all the rest and Coyote grew crazy in love with this star. He noticed the stars would pass by the top of a certain mountain. Coyote got it into his head that if he climbed the mountain, he would be able to reach out and touch the star.

He set off running, and maybe you've noticed this too—a mountain can seem close by, but as you start walking towards it, it seems further and further away. That's what happened to Coyote, and he was exhausted when he finally reached the mountain. He climbed to the top and waited. As night began to fall, Coyote was now so high up in the sky, he could see the stars just weren't walking across the sky—they were dancing!

He listened to their song, and called out to the Star Woman, asking her to let him come up into the sky and dance with them. "Oh, no, Coyote," she called down to him. "We're stars. We dance forever. Even if you did come up and dance with us, after awhile you'd just get tired and want us to let you back down again. Stay where you belong, Coyote. Don't try to be like us."

"Oh," cried Coyote,"I can dance forever, too!" And so it was the Star Woman reached down and grabbed Coyote's hand and pulled him up into the sky where they danced. They danced for a very long time, and Coyote grew tired and hungry. Finally they reached the very top of the sky where everything was bitter cold and silent. Coyote was miserable. "Please let me return to the earth," he begged her.

The Star Woman didn't say a word. She just let go of his hand and he fell. He was so high up in the sky, he fell for seven days and seven nights. He hit the top of the mountain so hard, he blew the top of it off. His blood turned to water and his bones turned to sand. These days we call where he hit Crater Lake. Nowadays White people say coyotes howl at the moon, but now you and I both know coyotes are scolding the Star Woman that killed their grandfather.

(A traditional Sahaptin story retold by Ty Nolan)

I began to travel early on in my educational career. I had been awarded a Ford Foundation Fellowship for American Indians and had been accepted into a Ph.D. program in Comparative Mythology at UCLA. I thought this would be a good way to study legends in an effective and supportive environment.

However, I received a ton of recruitment mail from Universities across the country, since it turned out the Ford Foundation Fellowship was a "portable" one, which meant you could use it anywhere. I was certain I'd be at UCLA that fall, but a mimeographed pamphlet caught my eye, offering a Summer Institute in Indian Studies at the University of Washington. The premise was the University would bring in various Native Professors from colleges across the United States, and 28 Native graduate students recruited nationally.

During the nine weeks of the Institute, we would be taught how to teach Indian Studies on a college level. I went from never having had a Native teacher in the schools and colleges I attended to suddenly *only* having Native professors. During my first weeks there, the secretary of the Institute who was also with the Indian Studies Program literally dragged me by my wrist to the College of Education. The Center for Indian Teacher Education had just received a federal grant to hire five Native graduate students to serve as half-time staff for the Center, while completing Master's degrees in Education. This was a major turning point in my life, and I did not end up enrolling at UCLA the end of that summer, but stayed at the University of Washington, learning a great deal about curriculum design.

My specific role at the Center for Indian Teacher Education was to provide college level courses to American Indian reservations within a 90 mile radius of Seattle. This was one of the first times such courses were offered on-site, rather than requiring people to commute to Seattle. It was very popular and I would have extremely large classes of non-Native teachers wanting to do the requirements to keep their teaching credentials current and Native people from the reservations interested in the topic, and they knew they could apply the classes to a degree. I was teaching various classes in Native American Art.

A few years after I had completed a Master's in Higher Education and was no longer at the University of Washington, a Chinese-American friend of mine asked me to co-teach a college class in multi-ethnic cooking. We had worked together with an anti-racism and discrimination project in the public schools.

It was her idea food was something all people had in common—but foods differ across communities. People combine foods in different ways. Some foods are taboo. Some groups will serve something at the start of a meal, and another culture will serve the same thing at the end of one. Some cultures are appalled by the thought of cheese, and some cultures include dog in their diet. Even as I am writing this, there is an on-going controversy over the slaughter of horses for food. This used to be done in the United States, and horsemeat is a regular part of the diet in a number of cultures. It's the difference between seeing a horse as a pet, or as livestock. If you're curious, I've never eaten horsemeat.

A course in multi-ethnic cooking allowed us to approach cultures in a non-threatening way. And the best part—after discussing how foods are prepared and served, and telling the stories of how the food plays a role in the lives of a particular group—we were able to eat our lesson!

I also watched (and helped) my relatives prepare traditional foods for guests at the tribal resort. As I listened to them tell the legends that went with the foods being prepared, and the sacredness of the food—I always thought at one point I wanted to share that with other people.

Just so, this is my opportunity to remember a lot of those dishes and the stories that went with them. When you live in a reservation household with a lot of little Indian kids underfoot, you accept the fact when you're ready to run out the door to sing, you'll often reach for your drum and realize all your drum sticks are missing. Little kids love drum sticks. You end up playing your drum with a sock you wrapped around a wooden spoon.

Some of the recipes I'll share will be hard to duplicate unless you're able to find a patch of bitterroot, dig them up and dry them properly. Sometimes you have to metaphorically wrap a sock around a wooden spoon. There were times when someone showed up unexpectedly at the door, and my mom would grab a roll of Pillsbury biscuits and throw them into hot oil to do a very fast version of Indian Fry Bread. If you use the roll of biscuits, it makes a fairly good standard fry bread. If you use a package of crescent rolls, then you get a version of the sopapillas you'll find in New Mexico.

While I enjoy fixing something very traditional, I was taught never to be afraid of trying something new, so I try to be creative when I can. For example, we gather huckleberries at the end of summer as a traditional food. For a change of pace, I'll make huckleberry custard filling for cream puffs.

I'll also introduce you to the first step in preparing Moose Nose Soup, or what will happen if you harvest the wrong camas.

But I know by now you're expecting a Coyote legend:

Coyote and Salmon

Long time ago, when the world was new, Coyote was going along. Coyote heard the Beaver sisters had created a dam to block the water, trapping all the salmon for their own use. Now, Coyote was hungry for salmon, and he plotted about how to get all the salmon for himself, although he also figured he'd tell everyone else he was liberating the salmon so everybody could have them—not just the Beaver sisters.

When he saw their lodge, he started screaming and yelling and shouting: "Oh, it's the most amazing thing! Oh, it's incredible! I can't believe it!"

The sisters came out to see what was making him crazy. "What is it, Coyote?"

"Oh, It's...words can't begin to...never seen anything like it! Huge! Big! Amazing!" He kept jumping up and down and screaming! "And it's really far OVER THERE!" And just like that, the Beaver sisters were running in that direction.

Coyote chuckled to himself and went into their lodge to "borrow" some baskets to carry salmon. Now in those days, baskets were different than they are now. They had feet—like a duck. Baskets would follow you around if you told them to. Coyote ordered the baskets to follow him down to the water where he cut a switch out of willow. He ordered the baskets to dip themselves into the water and capture as many salmon as they could. One by one, the baskets jumped into the water and emerged full of water and salmon.

"Now march!" commanded Coyote. "Faster! Faster!" He realized he needed to get away before the Beaver sisters returned. When he felt

the baskets weren't going as quickly as he wanted, he beat them with the switch. They sped up, but as they waddled with their burden, the water began to splash out of them.

"Careful! Careful! Don't spill any water or the salmon will die!" Oh, he whipped those poor baskets with his switch of willow. They slowed down, attempting to hold each drop of water within.

"Too slow!" Coyote shouted. "Faster! Faster! The Beaver sisters will be back any minute!" And he beat those poor baskets!

Every time the baskets slowed down he beat them, and every time they sped up and splashed out water he beat them.

Finally the baskets just squatted down, and would not move no matter how much he yelled at them or beat them. Exhausted from his effort, Coyote collapsed on the ground. As soon as he dropped his switch, each basket took off as fast as it could, running away from Coyote. They ran in different directions, and as soon as a basket would come to a river, it would dump the salmon out

And that's why even today, there are certain types of salmon that will come up one river, but not another, depending on which river a basket dumped its treasure.

And Coyote was so angry, he shouted, "Today, I, Coyote declare a new law! From now on, baskets will no longer have feet!" And that's why even today—baskets don't have feet.

(A traditional Sahaptin story, retold by Ty Nolan)

- There are five species of salmon native to the Pacific NW. Different salmon do indeed spawn and return to certain rivers and not others. The first White people to arrive recorded that the salmon runs were so great, you could "walk across their backs."

- The legends say Coyote gave strict instructions about how the Salmon People were to be treated with respect, and if humans did not do so, the Salmon people would stop returning. It would seem the legends are very true, and the Salmon People have dropped in numbers to the extent restrictions are in place to prevent the fishing industry from overharvesting.

One of my favorite memories is the taste of salmon eggs that have been placed directly under a broiler—about 4 inches or so, and allowed to stay there until they change color to look like cooked egg whites—keep checking on them—they will only take a few minutes. The white is actually the protein albumin, and if you've grilled enough salmon, you'll recognize it as the thick white droplets that will ooze out when the salmon is ready to put on your plate.

The texture of the salmon eggs will be closer to cream cheese, but they will have a fresh and amazing flavor. Incidentally, there is a difference between "caviar"—the eggs of the salmon that are unfertilized, and "roe," the fertilized eggs and already laid eggs of the salmon. If you live near a place where people actually fish for salmon, for example, the Fishermen's terminal in Ballard, or the Pikes Place Market in Seattle, see about buying the salmon eggs directly—otherwise they will be incredibly expensive. The salmon eggs will be in large masses almost brick shaped—this is what I remember putting under the broiler.

Early on, I mentioned Moose Nose soup. One of the first things you need to do? First get a moose. If you don't have Sarah Palin to shoot one for you, do the best you can. Sarah Palin has claimed that aerial hunting is necessary to help poor Alaskans who need to hunt moose for food. But it costs $500/hr. to charter a bush plane—that can make moose by the pound very expensive. Actually, if you've never hunted very large animals like moose or elk, you've probably haven't given much thought of how you'd pack out an adult moose that can weigh up to 1500 pounds.

In all situations like this, there is a prayer and often a thanksgivings ceremony that is done to celebrate the animal person sharing itself with you. There is assurance that the death is not a wasted one, but the flesh will be used in a respectful way to feed one's family. In some communities, part of the animal will be left out as a gift to wolves. And if you're making Moose Nose soup? You kick the hell out of the nose—as soon as you can—this will result in a hemorrhage of the blood so the nose will be saturated before you cook it.

The soup is good, although I will admit looking at the moose nose hairs is a little off-putting for me. The experience of Moose Nose soup, raw caribou, seal meat, and whale blubber are all Alaskan memories. I think my biggest surprise was having an Inupiaq woman serve me whale blubber with soy sauce. I felt that was very multicultural. In case you're curious, whale blubber is extremely chewy.

I also mentioned being careful what camas you gather—you have to look at the camas patches while they are still flowering, since their roots look so much alike. Purplish blue—great taste. White flowers? Death Camas. Not recommended.

There is a family story passed down by my Twana relatives. Long ago there were two sisters, and they worked as maids to one of the White women in the area. The two sisters committed a crime, and feared they would be executed. When the police came for them, they found the sisters dead—they had committed suicide by eating Death Camas.

How Deer Came To Be

Long and long ago, before the World turned upside down, all the people were animals. But they didn't look like the animals we have today. They looked more like human people. It wasn't until later that The Changer came and gave everything a purpose and a reason for being—changed the course of rivers—made mountains, and gave animals the sizes and shapes they have today. Some say Coyote was the one who did this, and Coyote never denied it.

Now imagine that someone came by tomorrow where you worked and announced that The Changer was coming on Friday, and would change everything. Some of you would end up with wings, some with horns, and some with fins. You might act the way the People did back then.

Some feared the Change. Some looked forward to it, and others were indifferent. The Deer People were Warriors, and thinking like Warriors, they didn't want things to change. They wanted things to stay the way they were. Thinking like Warriors, they decided it would be best to kill The Changer, so He wouldn't be able to Change them.

They took bones and began to sharpen them into knives. As they sharpened the bone knives they chanted, "Memelos, Memelos, Dukweebah, Memelos, Memelos, Dukweebah," which means "Kill the Changer! Kill the Changer!"

Then they sang their Deer Song and danced. Instead of a drum, they used the clacking together of their bone knives to keep their rhythm. When they finished they again chanted to "Kill the Changer."

Now Someone was watching them and that Someone was the Changer.

"What a pretty song Someone is singing," He said. "Will you sing it for Me again?" The Deer Warriors looked at each other and agreed to sing their song again. They finished with the chant of "Kill the Changer!"—sharpening their bone knives.

"Give me those!" He commanded. He took away their bone knives and sliced open their hands and feet. "From now on, you will be called "Sway-shut," or Split-Foot. You will be Deer." He shoved the bone knives into their bodies, and even today, Native people will use that bone as an awl in making baskets.

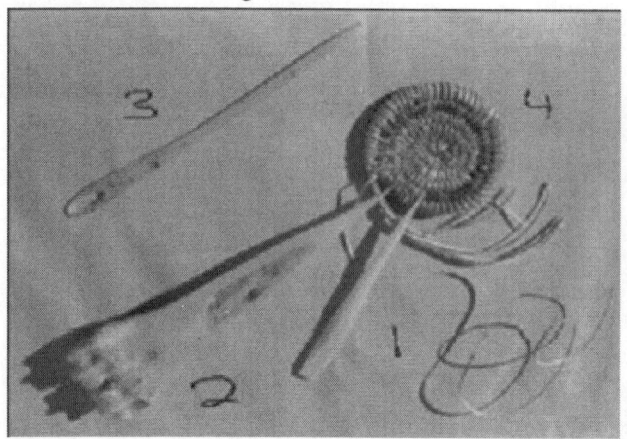

"Go forth—you will be Deer forever. And because you plotted to kill Me, you will be food for the Human People who are coming. They will use your skin for their moccasins, clothing and drums. They will use your hooves for rattles and your antlers. Every part of you will be used by the Human People who are coming. Now go!"

As they ran past Him, He clapped His hands twice to finalize the Change, and they all turned to look in the direction of the sound. Just so, even today, Deer will turn and look in the direction of a noise.

Further along the coast, they tell the story a little differently. They say that Deer sharpened knives made of shell.

When the Changer took the shell knives away, He stuck them on top of the Deer's head, and that's why even today, their ears are so *shell-shaped.*

It's also said that when He had finished, He noticed His hands were covered in white dust from the shells.

As the Deer ran by He slapped them on their asses, and that's why even today Deer has a white ass.

(A traditional Twana legend retold by Ty Nolan)

I tried to resist, but I have just spent too many years having to survive in Academia, so I feel obligated to point out this is an unusual Twana legend because the words of the song (gee, I should have done this as an audio book so I could just sing the songs, huh?) are not in Twana. They are actually in Chinook Jargon, the "trade" language of the Pacific NW that is a combination of a number of Native languages, French, Spanish, and English.

One year I was asked to review a book on Chinook Jargon by a University of Washington anthropologist. I went home to visit and was taking my Grandma Flora somewhere. We would be alone a long time in the car, so I asked her if she knew Chinook Jargon. She told me a story about her father that went on for the entire drive.

It involved her father being a Scout for the American army, and they were searching for Captain Jack. This is not the appropriate place for me to go into details, but let's just say Captain Jack was a chief of the Modoc people and American history can be quite messy. The bottom line is the federal government wanted him dead. Grandma Flora went into great detail about how her mother had made five pairs of moccasins for her husband, knowing he would be tracking Captain Jack across the lava beds, and their hard surface would wear out the moccasins. If only they knew about using ballet slipper soles in those days.

She described in detail what he saw and experienced. Finally, he encountered an old Indian man at the front of a cave. And at that point, she switched to Chinook Jargon and recounted their conversation. Captain Jack was hiding inside the cave, and that's how they captured him. Just so, Grandma Flora's father did single-handedly what required an entire team of Navy Seals and two helicopters to do the same thing with Osama bin Laden.

It was also an excellent example of an Elder taking nearly an hour to tell me a very complicated and involved oral history, rather than just saying: "Yes," when I asked her if she was familiar with Chinook Jargon.

This is also important to remember when you ask a traditional Elder a question you may not get the answer immediately. For example, as a young person, if you asked an Elder how to gather cedar bark in January, he or she might not respond, but on the hottest day of the summer, the same Elder would show up at your door and expect you to go with them to gather the cedar bark. One of the major differences between traditional Native education and conventional education is the separation that has occurred between learning and experience.

I can write down how to pick huckleberries for example, but words on a printed page or on an electronic device will only give you one level of information. If I take you out in August to gather huckleberries, you will hear different bird songs than you would have heard in January. You will see different things—smell different fragrances—around you. Traditional learning always would take place within the context of the reality.

The Twana legend always makes me think of deer jerky. Deer jerky is one of my favorite snacks. I would often come home from the University, and my mom would have strips of jerky drying above the stove.

Many legends like the one about Deer are told in a cycle during the Winter Time. Time in the world is understood to be in different stages. There is the time before The Change–the time during The Change–the time after The Change–and historical time. The actual word in the Twana language for The Change is *Spelatch*, which is the word used for "capsizing,"–like a canoe turning upside down. In the earlier times, forms were not as "set" as they are now, and people could more easily change back and forth between shapes. This is also why in Twana, when the English version begins "Before the World turned upside down," the actual word is *Spelatch*.

A great deal of the Northwest Coast Native Art explores this amazing transformation—one shape merging into another—the outer mask opens up and reveals a hidden mask within—here is an example of a Deer transformation mask:

Masks have a very special type of magic—they help you to see the world in a different way.

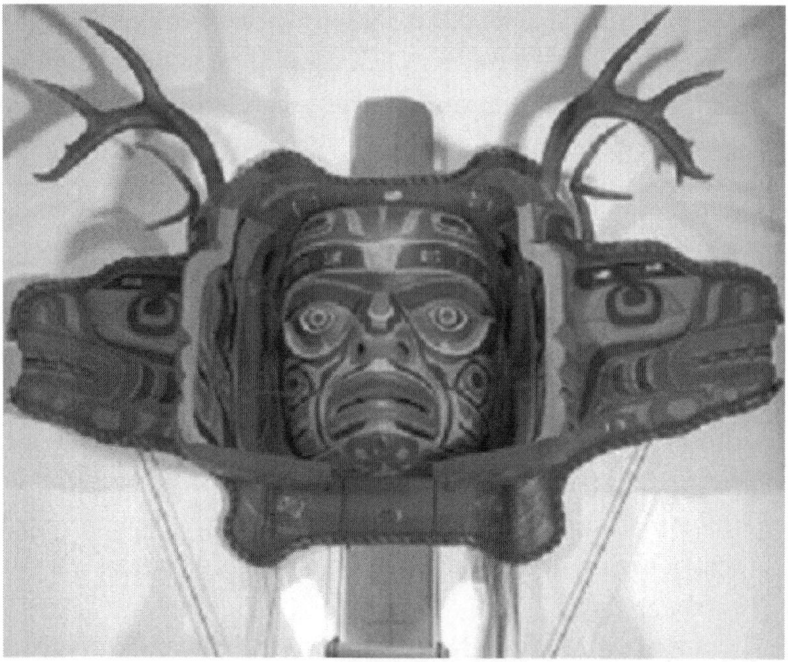

Chapter Two

As I begin Chapter Two, I want to emphasize I did not intend to create something where in addition to sharing stories, my secondary focus would be on how much baking powder will make the best fry bread, or how many cups of berries you should use to make *Wojapi*.

I'm from one of those families where no one ever measured anything and unlike all the competitive cooking shows I watch on television, we never had a magic kitchen where there was an unlimited supply of ingredients. Sometimes you simply ran out of enough smoked salmon and dinner tasted different that night than it normally did.

I grew up where you "eye-balled" things and compensated if you were running low on something. When a non-Native linguist came to write down the language, one of my aunts told him he'd never really understand the words unless he knew the culture, and he could never understand the culture unless he lived it. In the Zen tradition, this translates as "chop wood and carry water."

That reminded me of one of my favorite quotes from Ed Koch: "I can explain it to you, but I can't comprehend it for you." For example, if my Twana relatives were to say, "He hops like a jay," it indicates the person is a thief, but if you don't know the legend the phrase references, you won't "get it."

One year, a linguist was interviewing my relative, Georgie Miller. He asked her what the Twana word "spoh-ooch" meant. It was one of those very rare times when she suddenly went very polite. "It means passing wind," she said, demurely. It actually means "fart."

He wrote down it meant "breeze."

Oh, that reminds me of a story from my Pueblo relatives—Coyote was watching the sacred Katsina dancers in their ceremony, and noticed there was a lot of food they had prepared that was down below from where Coyote was on the top of the mesa. He summoned all of the other coyotes (in the Southwest, sometimes you end up with a whole herd of coyotes, so there's Blue Coyote, Spotted Coyote, Red Coyote—a sort of trickster family reunion).

He told them—"I've got an idea. We will make a living chain of coyotes!" (Yeah, what could possibly go wrong with that?) He instructed them to line up and everyone would bite the tail of the one in front of him. Then they would lower the chain of coyotes until Coyote could reach the food. He would grab it and then the rest of them would pull him up.

Everyone chomped on the tail of the coyote in front of him, and carefully they lowered each other down the side of the mesa. About halfway down, one of them farted.

"Who farted?!" yelled one of them. Of course, he had to open his mouth to say this, so the rest of the chain of coyotes fell to their (temporary—it's really hard to kill one in the legends) deaths.

So—here are some more stories, and here are some more recipes—and maybe, just maybe, you'll find a few of my memories. I should also warn you. Here's the thing about Storytellers.

For a lot of Native people there is a distinction made between stories and Stories, or perhaps it would be better to explain in English—a difference between Oral History and Oral Tradition. To put it another way, the wonderful Isabel Allende said in an interview she was a liar—because that was the definition of a Storyteller.

For a lot of us, we are required to formally introduce a Story to indicate to an audience if they need to listen with their ears, or with their hearts. Oral History means you pay attention to specific details. When the Federal Boldt Decision on Native Treaty Fishing Rights was made in 1974, Native Elders had testified as to where the government officials stood during the signing of the treaty, what time of day it was, and what direction the wind was blowing.

They quoted what was negotiated, and that was confirmed by the notes that were taken by Governor Steven's staff at the time. Not a single one of these Elders had been born at the time of the 1855 treaty signing.

But there are other Stories that are told as teaching stories, where the time of day, or the direction of the wind isn't really the issue. For some memories, will I remember things exactly the way someone standing next to me at the time will remember the event twenty or forty years later? Probably not.

I'm also worked for a number of years as a journalist. For that reason, if I mention the earliest complete set of a Bone Game (a Native Tradition) found is over 14,000 years old, I will go ahead and link you to an independent source, so you don't think I'm just imagining it. But if I tell you Grandma Flora sat on a suitcase in our front yard as a hint she wanted someone to take her somewhere—I can't link you to the proof.

But she did. One time I went to her and said, "Where do you want to go, *Kussa?*" (Grandmother)

She said, "I wanna go tomorrow."

I replied, "That's not a problem. I'm here all weekend. You just tell me where you want to go."

"I wanna go tomorrow."

I got frustrated. "I'll be happy to take you—you just need to tell me where."

It turns out there was a little town near The Dalles in Oregon named Morrow. It was where her checks were mailed. So, I took her to Morrow that day.

Did that exchange with my Grandma Flora really happen? It sure did, and I took her to her little place in Morrow and for the first time in my experience, she walked across her floor without using her cane. But you know the important thing about Stories? Even if it didn't "really" happen, it should have.

So, with that in mind, let me tell you a Story.

Abalone Girl and Gold Girl

Long time ago, when the world was still new, Coyote had a son. Now Coyote's son was so handsome—so good looking, that whenever he walked by, women (and some men) would feel their hearts beat faster. In fact, Coyote's son was so fine, you might even call him a fox.

Now in those days there were two sisters. Abalone Girl and Gold Girl. "Perhaps," Abalone Girl told her sister, "if we dress up in our very best clothes..."

"—And paint our faces," added Gold Girl, "maybe Coyote's son will fall in love with us!" Just so, they put on their best white buckskin dresses. They carefully painted each other's faces, and had just finished when they heard their grandmother's voice.

"What are you doing?" She asked.

"We thought if we dressed in our finest and painted our faces, Coyote's son might fall in love with us."

Their grandmother looked sad, and she told them, "Come here—there is something I must do first.' She reached down and dug her fingers into the earth, and began to smear her granddaughters with mud and dirt.

"Oh, Grandmother, what are you doing!?"

"If Coyote's son is a good person," she told them as she rubbed the mud into their hair, "he won't care about the way you look or how you dress. But if he is not a good person, then he will point his finger at you and laugh."

The sisters thought this was very strange, but you don't argue with your grandmother. They walked to Coyote's lodge, where his son was busy posing around so people could admire him. He looked up and saw two young women coming towards him. They were dressed in beautiful white buckskin dresses and bright paint was on their faces, but he could barely see it through the mud and dirt that covered them. He thought this was the funniest thing in the world.

He began to laugh and pointed his finger at the sisters. In many Native cultures, it is considered to be a bad thing to point your finger at someone. A polite person points with his or her lower lip. For some Native communities, the only time you point at something is to when you intend to kill it.

The sisters turned around, their hearts breaking. They knew that Coyote's son was not a very good person, but they were still hurt.

Abalone Girl cried and cried. She cried so hard her tears washed away all the mud and the dirt on her, but her tears also caused the colors she had painted on herself to run together. That's why even today when you see an abalone shell, the colors have run together.

Gold Girl did not cry tears of water, but of gold nuggets. The Elders tell us when you find gold nuggets—you know that Gold Girl

walked that way.

Even today, when you find abalone or gold nuggets, they are covered in dirt and mud, but beneath they have such great beauty. One of the reasons we tell this Story is to remind us humans are the same way—you need to look for their inner beauty, and not be distracted by what you may first see.

(A traditional Sahaptin story retold by Ty Nolan)

Abalone shell has been a traditional type of "money" that was traded all the way from Mexico and southern California where the larger, heavier, and more iridescent abalone originates, then further into British Columbia and Alaska. Native artists have long loved to use abalone shell as insets into art, masks and jewelry. In the Pacific Northwest where this legend is told, the native abalone is smaller with a more delicate shell that has paler colors.

Sadly, the native abalone is now endangered, so if you're going to enjoy some, make sure you use the more commercialized southern abalone. After you've cleaned it, you'll need to slice it into thin segments of a quarter of an inch or just a little thicker. Cover the meat with plastic wrap and then beat it to tenderize.

Afterwards it's a simple matter to sauté the slices in butter in a hot pan. Do it quickly—like a lot of seafood, if you overcook it, your delicacy will be tough and tasteless. It's a delight to then serve them in the original abalone shells.

Since I'm currently living in the Valley of the Sun (which beats the hell out of saying I live in the suburbs of Phoenix), I suspect it will be awhile before I have fresh abalone.

There's another legend that tells Coyote's son did not end up with a "happily ever after." He climbed up into a tree and fell, his long raven-bright hair tangled in the branches trapping him and so he died.

When Coyote found him, he mourned his child's death, and declared that in memory of his son, the hair tangled in the trees would become a gift to Human People.

In English, this is a lichen that some call "witch's hair," (talk about stereotypes!) You'll often find it referenced as black lichen, or sometimes horsehair lichen. It looks a lot like the Spanish moss in more southern and eastern communities, but it's not really a moss.

In Sahaptin, the lichen is called "*koonts*" (which is how you'll usually see it spelled, but it sounds more like "*kuntchz*"), which actually means "hair." It will grow on juniper, pine, and fir. It's gathered and carefully cleaned. Using long sticks that are curved at the end, the harvesters twist the long strands of the lichen and pull them down. The preparation and processing takes about 12 hours, and involves soaking it in water until it condenses and is less bulky.

The *koonts* is placed in the bottom of an earthen barbecue pit a couple of feet deep. Pine boughs are placed over a layer of rocks that have been heated in a fire, and then a layer of dry pine needles go over the green boughs, followed by the wet *koonts* in a burlap bag. There's another layer of boughs and pine needles, another clean burlap bag, and then it's all covered with a layer of soil. A long stick is positioned in the center and then removed—leaving a "hole" where water is poured into the pit and the hole will then allow steam to escape.

When it's done, the *koonts* will have further condensed into a brick like form, which is then cut into smaller "loaves" that can be stored for a long time.

To be honest, in Sahaptin tradition, this is considered a "famine food,' rather than something eaten on a regular basis. In more northern Native Nations, it's considered a delicacy. This may relate to the lichen taking on different flavors of its area. I've never had it outside of Oregon or Washington State.

For some of the "high" Feast Days in the Longhouses, Elders may prepare *koonts* to serve with the other traditional foods as part of the "thanksgivings ceremonies." The *koonts* bricks are soaked in water and prepared as a type of thin "pudding." While the brick is black, the pudding is a dark grey-green. The lichen is also traditionally used as a dye, which results in a dark green. The soaking of the lichen in water helps dilute its vulpinic acid which improves the taste—and too much vulpinic acid can be toxic.

How Raven broke Salmon Woman's Heart

Long and long ago, even before the world turned upside down, Raven was flying high and saw a beautiful woman with bright red hair. As he watched, she adjusted wonderfully fat fillets of salmon, hanging them to dry.

Raven's mouth began to water at the thought of all that salmon, and he swooped down to court her. In those days, People could shift back and forth from one form to another. He landed on the ground to stretch out his wings and took on human form.

He told her how her eyes sparkled like sunlight on water, and how amazing her hair was.

Raven can be charming when he wants to be and soon Salmon woman offered him a meal of the most delicious salmon he had ever had.

Days stretched on and Raven settled into a happy state of a full stomach and endless salmon. One night as he curled beside her, he told her how much he envied her bright red hair that flashed like the fire beside them.

"If you wish," she smiled, "you can have hair like mine." So saying she began to sing and stroked his head with fingers she had dipped into the icy water of the basket that she kept close to her bed. Magic flowed from her fingertips and soon Raven's head was covered in luxurious hair that matched her own.

Salmon woman would leave each morning to tend to the salmon, and vainly, Raven admired himself for hours in the shiny surface of a copper.

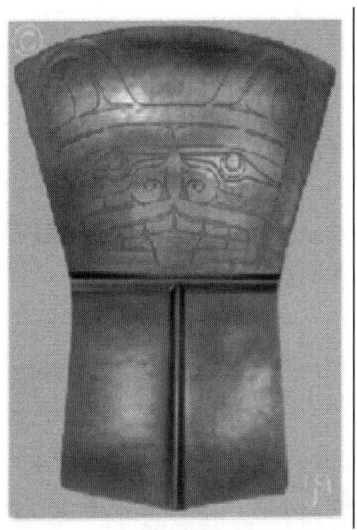

Copper is the name for the special objects made of copper that represent great wealth. Unlike most metals, copper can be used without being smelted, and is greatly loved by many Native people. And speaking of love, Raven loved the way he looked, and he reached for a piece of salmon that was hanging by the fire. Not watching, he accidently knocked the salmon down and into the ashes of the fire.

He sneered at the marred salmon, and then laughed because everywhere he looked there was more salmon, just waiting. Just so, he kicked the fallen salmon into the fire.

For Native people, food is Sacred, and in the Northwest, salmon is said to be the first food given by the Creator to Human People. When it is eaten, it is felt to be like the Eucharist for Christians—it is a type of communion with the Sacred. It is treated with such respect that many Northwest Nations still observe a First Salmon Ceremony. This is when the very first salmon of the run is caught and praised as one of Noble Birth.

The body of the First Salmon is grilled over a open fire, with the head, tail, and skin saved. The Elders of the community are offered the flesh of this Salmon, and then the remains are placed on a tray of ferns and a procession forms, with the remains carried to the river where it spawned, while members of the community sing a song of thanksgivings.

The salmon returns at death to the river that spawned it, thus completing its circle. The Elders say if this ceremony is not performed, the Salmon People will stop returning.

The Salmon woman walked into her lodge just in time to see Raven callously kick her precious salmon into the fire as if it were simply trash. Heartbroken, she turned and walked away, silent as the stones. Her tears fell with silence heavier than the stones.

As she walked outside, the salmon began to move. Even the salmon that had been drying began to twitch and switch. Every salmon, even the one covered in ashes, came back to life and followed her and her tears to the shore.

Raven called out his apologies, but she ignored him, and stepped into the dark water. The salmon splashed into the river, causing a great boiling of water.

Raven watched them disappear and suddenly his scalp began to itch like crazy. He touched his head and clumps of red hair fell out and onto the ground. The only thing left were the stiff black feathers Raven wears today.

Some say the Salmon woman was so hurt by what Raven had done, she will only near the shore in the form of mist or fog, where she swirls and dances and listens to discover if the Human People are treating her children with respect.

(A traditional Twana story retold by Ty Nolan)

Two nights ago I baked a sockeye salmon, laid upon slices of lemon I had placed in the center of heavy duty aluminum foil. I lightly salted and peppered the top of the salmon, splashed in fresh lemon juice and then tightly sealed the foil. I had placed the aluminum foil package on a new cookie sheet and put it into the oven at 400 degrees.

I had also made a matching sealed envelope of foil that I had filled with raw peeled shrimp, roasted garlic, and basil straight from the pot on my patio, kernels I had cut from a fresh ear of corn, and a few splashes of chili sauce. I squeezed more fresh lemon juice on top, before I had placed it into the oven. I checked on both occasionally until they were done.

I enjoy the idea of taking traditional Native American foods—in this case, the shrimp, fresh corn, and chili—but in a new combination, since Native people from the Southwest would be used to corn and chili, but historically would rarely encounter shrimp. In Pacific Northwest traditional cooking, strong spices are not used. But I enjoy spicy things so two days later I took the leftover salmon from the refrigerator and simmered it in a tasty salsa after I had sautéed garlic and onion in the pan first.

For color and crunch, during the last few minutes of cooking, I threw in a handful of diced green pepper. Just before I was ready to use the salsa salmon filling, I scattered in a handful of shredded parmesan cheese to thicken the mixture.

Meanwhile, I had taken taco shells and first swiped the inside with sour cream, then a dollop of guacamole in the center. I took an additional sliver of fresh avocado and laid it on top of the guacamole, and then squeezed fresh lime juice over the guacamole/avocado. I filled the taco shells with the salsa salmon and sprinkled shredded lettuce on top. A very tasty and juicy way to end a busy day.

Why Rabbit Has Paws Instead of Fingers

Long time ago, even before the world turned upside down, Rabbit loved to gamble. Now there was one thing Rabbit loved to do even more than gamble—he loved to cheat.

Like many Human People these days in the Pacific Northwest, Rabbit played Bone Game. This is also called "Stick Game," "Hand Game," or *S'lahal*. In the Salish language, S'lahal translates as "Bone."

Our stories say that Bone Game was a gift from the Creator, designed to settle disputes in a peaceful, rather than a violent manner. The oldest set of the Bone Game found so far is at least 14,000 years old.

I was also taught that traditional healing is related to the Bone Game. A medicine person is "betting" his or her Power to heal is greater than the power of the disease to kill. This means a healer is, in essence, betting his or her life against the life of the patient's. This is why in many Native communities—a healer has four days to make the decision whether or not to treat a patient.

It gives the healer the opportunity to determine if his or her power is an appropriate one for a particular disease. If not, a healer may refer to someone else. I guess the most important thing is to realize a gambling activity like the Bone Game also has a strong spiritual aspect to it.

Traditionally the playing pieces are made from deer bones. It was also played with cougar bones, and there used to be an old woman near the Lummi Indian reservation who was said to play with a set made from human shin bones. Nobody liked to play with her...

The bones are marked—there are two sets. One bone is "belted" with a stripe carved or colored into it around the middle. Its mate will have no stripe. One is considered male and the other female. The other side tries to guess which hand is hiding the bone with no stripe.

The pieces are small enough to be hidden within the hand. In more modern times, other materials are used in their construction—for example, Lucite, plastic, or wood.

A deer bone like this would be cut in half, and then a set of matched bones would be made from the halves, cutting them down further and then marking one as male and leaving the other unmarked as a female bone.

The score is kept by counting sticks. Each side of players has an equal number of sticks, and then one side will start with the additional "kick" stick or "king" stick. The king stick is like the king in chess. Every time a side incorrectly guesses the location of the unmarked bone the guessing/pointing side will give up a stick to the other side.

Every time a side correctly guesses which hand is hiding the unmarked bone, the hiding side will turn over that set of bones to the guessing team. When both sets of bones are won, then the teams change positions in terms of which one will hide and which one will guess/point. The game is played until the king stick is won.

It is said there are at least nine different ways that you can cheat playing Bone game.

Rabbit knew every single way. Just like there are "double-sided coins," where the coin is the same on both sides, one way Rabbit would cheat was to paint the stripe only halfway around the bone. When the other side would guess him, he would turn the cheating bone to show the "wrong" side.

Now in those days, Rabbit had fingers, just like you and me. He also had a long bushy tail like a squirrel, but that's another legend.

When you play Bone game, it's not unusual for players to do a sort of "hand dance," moving the hands around in rhythm to the Bone game songs that are being sung. The player will hold a bone piece between index finger and thumb, so everyone can see it. Hand drums, rattles, and sticks beaten against other sticks keep the rhythm going. The hand gestures are saying, "look how well I'm playing—you'll never guess where I'm hiding the bones—are they here? Are they there?—you'll never guess me!"

Sometimes a player will keep switching the bones around behind a drum until she is ready to hold up her hands. Sometimes a player will keep switching the bones around behind another player until ready to hold up his hands. Sometimes a player will keep switching the bones beneath a shawl or a blanket until she's ready to hold up her hands, both clutching one of the matched bones.

One day Rabbit was playing Porcupine. "You better not be cheating on me, Rabbit."

"Me!? Cheat you!?, You Porcupine!" And then Rabbit would cheat him again.

Porcupine had a very special Spirit Power—he could call lightning down from the sky.

He began to sing his Power song, and as he struck his drum harder with his stick, the clouds began to darken the sky. There was the sound of thunder, and then lightning flashed down so close to Rabbit, it burned all the hair out of the inside of his ears.

That's why even today when you see a rabbit—it has no hair inside its ears.

But Rabbit kept cheating.

Porcupine grew more angry. He began to sing his Power song again, as Rabbit proudly did his hand dance, showing off the bones he had won by cheating. Lightning flashed down from the sky and blew all the fingers off the hands of Rabbit.

That's why even today when you see a rabbit—it has paws instead of fingers.

But STILL Rabbit was cheating. Now Rabbit had a very special place to hide his bones...not underneath his drum—not behind another player—not beneath a shawl–he hid them up his nose.

This time, Porcupine didn't even sing. He lifted his hand up towards Rabbit, and lightning shot right out and hit Rabbit in the nose until his bones fell out on the ground.

That's why even today when you see a rabbit, it has such a flat, funny, and boneless nose.

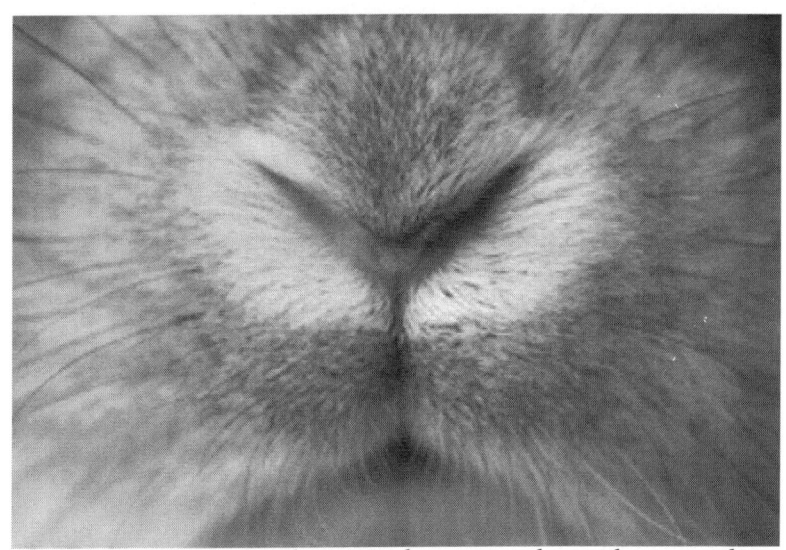

And that's why even today—you better not cheat when you play Bone Game!

(A traditional Sahaptin Story retold by Ty Nolan)

Rabbit can be a tasty addition to the menu, although for many urban dwellers, it is unlikely rabbit will be found at the local grocery store.

Fortunately there are specialty stores that will carry rabbit (often frozen) and with the internet, you can buy almost anything.

As a small child, I remember my family having cages with rabbits in the "backyard" but it was a long time before I made the connection that the rabbit I had slipped a carrot the day before was on the table the next evening.

Of course, the easiest way to get a rabbit is to have a family member who is a hunter, who then cleans and dresses the rabbit for you.

In some communities, there are rabbits, but there are also hares, which tend to be larger and longer limbed than a rabbit. A jackrabbit, for example, is really a hare. In more northern areas, you'll find the snowshoe rabbit, which is also actually a hare.

Rabbits tend to be a little "tough" so if you do not have to cook one over a fire while camping, a lot of recipes will stew or braise the meat in order to tenderize it. In my experience teaching multi-ethnic cooking at Seattle Central Community College, I sometimes found non-Natives who got a little freaked out by "wild" meats that they automatically assume would taste "gamey."

What's funny to me is that asking if these folks had ever tasted "wild" meat before—they hadn't, which means they really didn't have a personal point of reference as to what a "gamey" flavor would be in the first place. I suppose they define "gamey" as "not tasting like chicken."

For that reason, rabbit can be prepared by marinating and cooking it in wine, beer, vinegar, or in a chili stew base, which will tend to overcome the direct taste of the rabbit, if you are concerned with squeamish guests.

Let's face it—after a lifetime of Bugs Bunny, Peter Cottontail, and the Easter Bunny, rabbit on the menu is a really hard sale if you're expecting small children around the dinner table. I'll admit as a youngster I didn't notice the "drumstick" I would enjoy didn't really look anything like a chicken leg but hey—I'm not the sharpest spoon in the drawer, and a lot of other children will figure that out long before I did.

That's why cooking the rabbit until the meat falls off the bone is an excellent way to avoid identifiable body parts you have to explain to horrified children or adults.

Did I mention you used to be able to buy a t-shirt on my mom's reservation that read: "Vegetarian is the Indian word for *Poor Hunter.*"

I used to do what I watched my relatives do, which is to dredge the meat in flour mixed with a little salt and pepper—the way we would do most meats—beef, elk, deer, or chicken. But I caught one of the American Test Kitchen shows and they did a comparison of pot roasts where the meat was dredged in flour before browning, and where the meat was not, and both methods produced fairly identical results.

Since then I've saved a step and given up on the flour dredge. I just brown the meat directly in the skillet or the Dutch oven I'll be using to do a "one pot" meal.

I'll then add enough water to cover the meat, and let it simmer away for 30 or 45 minutes (If I'm cooking in the evening, then I check during commercial breaks...'cause I'm not an "urban Indian"—I am a "urbane Indian" lol)

After spicing the liquid with salt, black pepper, and at least a teaspoon of crushed red pepper, I'll also add some garlic and whatever fresh herbs are available on my patio. When the meat has had a "head start," I'll add some diced cabbage.

This is also the standard way my Tiwa relatives will do a pork cabbage stew back home at the Pueblo, although they'll skip the garlic and herbs, but will also sometimes use roasted green chilies as opposed to the crushed red chili powder. If I'm feeling fancy, I'll also throw in some diced white onion, because I think onion goes well with the cabbage, garlic, and rabbit.

Keep checking between commercials to see when you're satisfied the rabbit is tender enough, poking it liberally with a sharp knife or a fork. Depending on various factors like how much rabbit you're using, sunspots, and rogue moons crossing your major sun signs, the cooking time will be roughly an hour and a half to two hours.

Serve a bowl up with a slice of substantial and good crusty bread and no one will think of accusing you of "bunnicide."

Chapter Three

Let me emphasize I did not intend to create something where the primary focus was on how many ears of corn you will need to make kneel-down bread, or how many huckleberries should go into your pie.

While I will certainly share recipes with you, my intention is to weave together ideas about the role of foods in Native culture, and to share some of the legends I will often use when performing as a Storyteller that I think go with the food in a way you might pair a wine with a meal.

Origin of the Butterfly

Long and long ago, there were two caterpillar people who loved each other very much, but as with all living things, one of them died. The caterpillar woman mourned the loss of her husband. She didn't want to talk to anyone, didn't want to be around anyone. She wrapped her sorrow around her like it was a shawl and began walking.

All the time she was walking, she was crying. For twelve moons (one year) she walked, and because the world is a circle, she returned to where she had started. The Creator took pity on her and told her, "You've suffered too long. Now's the time to step into a new world of color — a new world of beauty." The Creator clapped hands twice, and she burst forth as the butterfly. Just so, for many Native people, the butterfly is the symbol for everlasting life and renewal.

(A traditional Sahaptin story retold by Ty Nolan)

Just as life repeats art, this legend sets a pattern the Sahaptin people use in accepting the loss of a loved one.

By the way, writing about the Butterfly legend was actually the first "official" (i.e., academic) publication I ever did, through the *University of Manitoba Medical Journal*. My mentor, Carolyn Atteneave, recommended me to take over her obligation to submit an article. Since then, I've tried to support her effort by asking others who are less experienced to work with me in publishing something professionally for periodicals, or textbooks.

I've done a great deal of work in the area of grief and loss. This was a particular issue before the current HIV medications became available. In the early days, care providers would often lose literally hundreds of patients to AIDS. The need was so great, the empty bed of a dead patient would be immediately filled by someone with the disease.

I was involved with two national projects. The one with the American Psychological Association eventually became known as Project Hope, and I was on the original curriculum design team. Project HOPE provided training for mental health professionals to improve their services to patients with HIV. I remember one of my team members was a social worker in D.C., and she shared she woke up one day and realized everyone she had on speed-dial had died of AIDS.

I also worked with Leon McKusick (we had both been with the APA Project). We provided workshops for two years for the HIV Frontline Forum. He had been the local coordinator for the International AIDS Conference when it had first been held in San Francisco. The next IAC was held in Amsterdam, and we did one of the primary keynotes, discussing our research on bereavement concerns for family, friends, and providers who had lost people to HIV/AIDS.

We had first presented our findings at an American Psychological Association conference. To be very brief—what seems to matter is that an individual actually "does" something to address their loss. But it doesn't seem to matter what that "something" might be. In other words, unlike a recipe for fry bread which will usually provide the same results each time, I can't prescribe someone who is grieving to do "x," based on what works for a member of my family, or for the social worker in D.C.

The important thing is what we call back home "intentionality." You announce to the Universe (and your heart) you are doing "this" and "this is what it means." For some people, that might be lighting a candle. For another it might mean putting a photo of the deceased in a special place. What matters is the grieving person needs to do *something*. I was trained by Elizabeth Kubler-Ross around death and dying issues. She told us: "You have a choice: you can suffer now, or you can suffer more later."

She meant when dealing with grief, you can address it right away, or you can delay the process, and that process will become even more painful by postponing it. I should also share that when Leon and I were doing grief and loss workshops for AIDS/HIV Service Organizations across the United States and Canada, even though we were specifically focused on loss from AIDS, everyone we saw would have "unfinished business" that had nothing to do with HIV.

In other words, the people in our workshops had never fully worked through the loss of a sibling, a grandparent, or another loved one. The AIDS losses simply stacked on top of that unfinished grieving.

With the workshops, I would share the Sahaptin traditions that follow the structure of the Origin of the Butterfly legend:

When a family member dies, a *Palaxsiks* is held. The mourning ceremony of the *Palaxsiks* follows the "map" of this legend. After the body has been buried, the surviving spouse, usually within a week of the burial, will be stripped of his/her regular clothing behind a blanket screen.

Relatives from one side of the family have brought new clothes of dark colors that are used to dress the widow/widower. This indicates the cocoon stage. The hair is cut. But since hair continues to grow, at one point, it will return to its original length. This external reality represents the psychological and spiritual healing that is taking place internally.

Incidentally, the cut hair and the dark clothing also serve to mark an individual in the mourning process, so community members can acknowledge this and act accordingly. However, when a non-Native client begins therapy, a provider will have no way of knowing if the client is experiencing bereavement until a history is taken, and even then it may not come up immediately.

At the end of one year, there is a closure ceremony where the family members who received the "grief" clothes during the first ceremony bring new clothes of bright colors to dress the widow/widower. The bright colors represent the wings of the butterfly and also signify that the time of bereavement is over, and the individual is freed of the restrictions of the previous year.

For example, when in mourning, an individual is not permitted to take part in social dancing. After the end of the year's observance, the headstone for the dead is usually placed. This led to an interesting discussions among Elders (I was too young at that point to be included) where there had been a significant death in our family, and two of my young nephews had been named as "American All-Stars" players for a national softball tournament. This, like many sports events, was considered a very great honor within a lot of Native communities.

Just so, it's very clear in our traditions, if your loved one has died, you are not permitted to take part in social (e.g., Powwow) dancing until after the mourning ceremony is over. There are also a lot of common restrictions, such as a new widow not being able to cook in the community kitchen, because it is believed she might add her sorrow to the food she was preparing.

Indeed, in the real tradition, during the time of grief, you would not be permitted to do most everyday activities—this not only included cooking but even washing your own hair. During the year of mourning, your extended family would do all that for you, so you could just concentrate on grieving. As you might imagine, moving into a cash-based economy made this sort of practice difficult.

But while not dancing in Powwows was well established as taboo, what sense did one make of a strictly non-Native practice, such as an All-Stars Softball Tournament? Being Native American can be complicated. Here was the solution the Elders shared: the two teenagers who had been named national "All-Stars" were given a private mourning ceremony to "release" them from their social obligations, since once one has gone through the mourning ceremony, your mourning is by definition, over. All the rest of the extended family needed to keep up the restrictions until the regular year period of grief was over.

I should probably mention there have been other alterations to the traditions due to non-Native influences on our realities. As a result, for a lot of families, the grief period has been reduced from a full year to three months.

One of the questions I often get asked at Grief and Loss workshops is how long the bereavement period should last. The answer is—"your mileage may vary." If you grew up in a household that gave you legends and dances and rituals that emphasized the mourning period lasted 12 moons, the chances are, you'd see 12 moons as "normal" for a time of grief. But a lot of non-Native people did not grow up with this message. Elizabeth Kubler-Ross offered up 18 months as an "average" time of grief. But that means the "average" indicates a number of people will require less than 18 months, and others will require more.

I was very moved when I was doing a Grief and Loss Workshop in Canada and had an elderly non-Native man approach me at the end of the presentation. "All the time people here have tried to comfort me, they told me to just *get over* my loss. I was married for over forty years. I can't *just get over it*. But you told me sorrow is like a load of stones blocking a road. You might just have to take away one rock at a time. I can't just wipe away my pain in one swoop. But I think I can take away one rock at a time."

Our Community members are exposed to the story throughout the year. Like many tribal nations, Sahaptin reservations will have dances that are considered "theirs" apart from the conventional "powwow" style competitive dancing that is acknowledged as "outside" and brought back during World War II where they were shared by Native soldiers from such places as Oklahoma.

Just so, one such traditional dance is the "*wilik wilik waashashat,*" or Butterfly Dance. It is performed by adolescent females who line up single file. They pull their colorful fringed shawls over their heads and begin to cry out loud as they walk in a circle. Again, this represents the cocoon period.

The head drummer carefully watches, and when the lead dancer completes a circle, he or she will strike the drum twice. This is signal for the dancers to spread their shawls across their shoulders.

They then begin a skipping dance as the song's rhythm changes from its mournful march to a bright pattern. The legend is often told as part of the performance. Just so, Community members grow up hearing the legend told repeatedly, even when there are no deaths to be observed. As a result, the knowledge of how to properly mourn is passed on so when a family must deal with death, the members know how to do so.

After the *Palaxsiks* is performed, a feast is provided to those who attend. Over the years (in my experience) as more and more Latinos have come into the Pacific Northwest as migrant workers and have intermarried with Native people, it's now common for tamales to be served, along with more traditional foods, such as salmon or elk meat.

Cooking for someone you love is, from a Native American perspective, a sacred process. In earlier writings I mentioned the closest to "home style" canned salmon I've found is at Whole Foods—Copper River Salmon. The Whole Foods that is within walking distance of where I currently live in Tempe, Arizona, carries strips of smoked salmon that are sometimes called "Indian Candy" or "Salmon Candy."

They really do taste like what I'm used to on the reservation. I've also used leftover salmon I've baked, but the slightly smoky flavor really compliments Alfredo sauce. In full disclosure, I should point out I've never been served smoked salmon Alfredo on the reservation, even at the luxury resort.

Here's a quick and easy recipe. Take about 8 ounces of fettuccine pasta that you place in boiling water for about 12 minutes or so, checking to see if it's al dente, and then drain it.

In a sauce pan, plop a stick of butter along with a couple of chopped garlic cloves, browning the garlic to fully release its flavor. Blend in a cup of heavy cream, along with a few sprinkles of black pepper. Mix in a tablespoon of flour to help thicken the sauce and then gradually add a cup of grated Parmesan. Crumble 8 ounces of salmon, along with a couple of spoonfuls of capers.

If you like, you can also toss in a cup of fresh spinach. I always keep fresh basil in my garden to add another level of flavor. Stir it all together for 3-5 minutes, until everything is fully heated and toss with the pasta. We also enjoy artisan crusty bread with a splash of balsamic vinegar and olive oil as a side—it's great to dip into the sauce.

Why Blue Jay Hops

One of the last times I heard my relative Sobiyax (Bruce Miller) tell a story was at a conference in Las Vegas. He was in a wheelchair and looked frail. I still thought of him as being so large and strong. He had once punched out a horse. He broke his hand. When our van was blocked by a car that had parked too close, he managed to push it so hard, it tipped enough for us to back out.

Diabetes had taken away one of his legs; a stroke would take his life a few months later. At the conference, Sobiyax told the Twana story of "Why Blue Jay Hops." He also introduced me and told the audience I was his brother, and had the right to tell his family stories.

Long ago, long before the coming of the Great Flood, Blue Jay was hungry. He was excited to hear Bear inviting people to his Longhouse for a feast.

The food was placed in the proper ceremonial way, but there was no oil. Now in those days, one would dip one's food in oil, much the way today you might spread butter on your bread, or put dressing on your salad.

When the people saw there was no oil, they started to mutter, "Why Bear doesn't even know how to give a feast!"

Another commented, "No Oil! How Rude. We should just go home."

Bear heard what they said, and laughed. "You want oil?" he called out. "I'll give you oil!" And he danced out to the middle of his Longhouse where the fire was burning and the salmon was roasting.

He sang his Song and as he sang he rubbed his hands together. Now bears have a lot of fat underneath their skin, and the heat of the fire started to make the fat melt, and it dripped out in the form of oil. This was caught by his relatives in a large wooden bowl and they passed this around to his guests.

Someone was watching this and that someone was Blue Jay. He envied the Power and magic of Bear. Before the people left, Blue Jay called out, saying, "Next full moon, I invite all of you to my Longhouse for a feast!"

The following moon, the people gathered at the home of Blue Jay. Once again, they were shocked to see there was no oil.

"Blue Jay doesn't even know how to give a feast!"

"How rude! No oil! We should just go home."

Blue Jay laughed and shouted, "You want oil? I'll give you oil!" And he danced out to the middle of his Longhouse, where the fire was burning. He sang the stolen Song of Bear, and began to rub his hands – really his feet – together over the fire in the manner of Bear.

Now our Old People teach us that everyone has a Song. Part of becoming an adult is learning what your Song is, so you can become all that you can be. A Song can be given; a Song can be shared. But a Song must never be stolen.

Someone was watching. And that someone was the Creator. The Creator was so angry, He made the fire jump up and it burned Blue Jay's feet. And that's why even today when you see a Blue Jay, his feet are dark and twisted, as though they've been burned in a fire.

A Blue Jay can't walk like a normal bird. It can only hop. Even today, Old People will say, "He hops like a Jay," which means the person they're talking about is a thief.

The Trickster best known to non-Natives is probably Coyote, but if you continue further up in the Pacific Northwest, Native people will tell Raven stories that sound very similar to those of Coyote. Among some of the Native communities in between, the stories will focus on Blue Jay, and away from the Coast, the Winter

Spirit Dances are sometimes called Blue Jay Dances.

In one story, Blue Jay rescues light, but in doing so, a door slams shut on his poor head, resulting in its odd flattened shape.

A resource I would suggest, not only for Native American material, is the NPR program, *Sound & Spirit*. Fantasy writer Ellen Kushner is the host and co-producer, and the program frequently features mythological themes. Go to the NPR site and then scroll down through the archived programs to discover a terrific show on Tricksters, as well as one on Native Americans, and yet another on Storytelling.

As for the next recipe I'd like to share, I would suggest a tasty smoked salmon spread. Sobiyax was very fond of this and would often sit watching television while sharing a version of this with friends and relatives, usually dipping into it with potato chips. I've also used it as a sandwich spread with various other items.

Take about ¼ cup of mayonnaise or Miracle Whip—oh, who am I kidding...use real mayonnaise—the salmon deserves it. Mix in at least 6 ounces of Smoked Salmon. For me, canned Smoked

Salmon was always "handmade." Sobiyax and others would work hard putting away dozens of jars to use through the year. Again—we live in the age of Internet shopping, so I'm sure you can easily track Smoked Salmon down.

Squeeze in about a teaspoon of lemon juice. I also sprinkle in a few drops of Frank's Red Hot, but hey—I was shaped by years in the American Southwest. Add a teaspoon of diced garlic, and mix in about as much Parmesan cheese (the stuff in that green can—you know the one I mean—will do) as you did the mayonnaise.

If it's a little too thick, you can add a splash of heavy cream, although I suspect Sobiyax would have just added some more mayo. Blend or mix it up – and as I've mentioned elsewhere, I'm not a big fan of smoothing everything out. I much prefer to see (and taste) chunks of the Smoked Salmon rather than having it all come out to the consistency of cream cheese.

How Daylight Came To Be

(Why Ant Has A Small Waist—this was the story I told for the 25th anniversary of Mr. Roger's television program)

Long, long ago, so long ago, there was no light, there was only darkness. In those days, the Ant people worked very hard. But sometimes they would go looking for food, and could not find their way home again.

Sometimes, they would hear heavy footsteps, and a monster would reach into their homes and steal and eat their babies, disappearing into the darkness again.

This monster was Tsimox, the Grizzly Bear. Even now, bears will sometimes dig up the nests of ants to eat their larvae.

There was one person, Ant Woman, who was smarter than all the rest. "If we had light, we could see to work. We could find our way home. We could keep watch for the monster Bear, who steals our children."

Ant Woman decided to go to the house of the Creator, and ask for light on behalf of her people. It was a long and dangerous journey. She did not know it, but Bear followed her, to see what she would do.

"Oh, Creator," she said, "give my people light, so we can see and work..."

But before she could finish speaking, Bear stepped in front of her, saying, "Don't listen to her! Don't give this little bug person what she wants! I want it to always be dark so I can sleep and be cool!"

The Creator replied, "There will be a contest—a dance contest—and the winner will get his or her desire."

This was the very first Powwow, when people came together to compete in dance. Just as now, people came from the four directions to see the dancing. They brought all sorts of food to share with one another.

As soon as Bear saw all the different types of food, he became very excited and began to eat.

But little Ant Woman fasted. She concentrated on praying on behalf of her people. She pulled her belt tight around her waist, so she would not feel hungry. Finally it came time for them to compete.

She stood up, and told the people, "I am Ant Woman—I dance for light!" And then she did a fast dance, pulling her belt tighter and tighter.

When she had finished, Bear stood up and wiped the crumbs from his lips, saying, "I am Bear—I dance for night!" Then he did his slow and lumbering dance. When he had finished, he went back to eating.

For what we would now call seven days and seven nights they danced against each other. Ant Woman did not eat during this time, continuing to fast and pray. She pulled her belt tighter and tighter.

Bear stood up to dance against her, but he was now so fat and full, he could hardly move. He was so tired and sleepy… "I am Bear…I dance for…" and then he fell asleep right in the middle of his dance. He began to snore loudly.

"Little Ant has won," said the Creator, "but both the Ant and Bear are my children and I love them both. For that reason I will give them both what they wish for—daylight for the Ant People so they can see and work, and night time for the Bear, so he can sleep and be cool."

And so it is today we have day and night because of the wonderful little Ant Woman. And if you see an ant today, you'll notice she pulled her belt so tight, she still has a tiny waist, so you know this story is true. In the Twana language, the name for ant is "tlatlusid" which means "tied or cinched at the waist."

(A traditional Twana story, retold by Ty Nolan)

This is a lovely little story that has a lot of memories for me. Many years ago, several of us were involved with something called the *Indian Readers Series*, which was a project out of the NW Regional Educational Laboratory. A number of American Indian reservations in the Pacific NW designated American Indian storytellers and artists to put some of their traditional legends into booklets that were geared to the reading levels of various grades.

My major objection to this was the fact the oral comprehension level of young children will be higher than their reading comprehension. As a result, this story, which was retold and illustrated by my relative, Bruce Miller, had to be restructured to a Kindergarten reading level, which lost a lot of its intricacy. I did the illustrations for a couple of other books in the series. I had always wished the laboratory had made audio recordings to supplement the material designed for the lower reading levels.

At one point, a dear friend of mine, Vi Hilbert, was doing American Indian storytelling demonstrations in her Native language of *lushootseed*. She saw me in the audience, and asked if I would come up and help her tell the story with her son, Ron.

If you are more familiar with NW culture, the story then carries many more layers of meaning. One of the most important elements of the tradition among the Salish people is the Winter Spirit Dance, which incorporates the Vision Quest familiar to a number of Native Nations. This can then be understood as part of what Ant Woman is doing—her focus on prayer and fasting.

In a number of Native communities, there is also the tradition of asking something from the Creator (health and recovery for a beloved, or in Ant Woman's example—help for her community) and an offer to give something of oneself. In the initiation process, it is not unusual for the person undergoing the ceremony to have a woven woolen sash or belt that is tied around the waist.

When the person ceremonially dances, he or she will have helpers who will hold on to the belt and pull against it, helping to strengthen the dancer. The initiation process, at least the Vision Quest aspect of it, often lasts for four days, although there are other legends and teachings about how someone may have one last much longer, or for a shorter period.

Different Nations have different versions of this legend. One of my Aunts used to tell the *Sahaptin* version, where it wasn't only Ant and Bear who danced—it was several different animals, each hoping for something special. For example, Rabbit danced so it would always be springtime, so he would have tender green things to eat. He lost the contest, but the Old People say that you can still hear rabbit thumping on the ground—which means he's practicing his dance, so next time he'll win.

Just so, Ant Woman didn't dance by herself, but with her relatives—the other insects with small waists, like the Wasp. But she was worried about the fact she and her relatives were so small and were surrounded by animal people like Bear, who might be sore losers. From Ant Woman's perspective, it would be very easy for the larger Animal People to stomp on them and turn them into grease spots. Thus, she came up with a plan.

Historically, the "big" annual powwow would end with a version of this legend. A group of young people would be chosen and would start off a round dance in the middle of the powwow grounds. The legend says Ant Woman told her audience, "As long as I am singing, you must look as angry as you might feel about losing the contest. You must look mean and heartless. Under no circumstances may you smile. But when the song stops, you have to turn to someone near you, point your finger at them and laugh. It can be the low deep laugh of Bear, or the high squeaky laugh of Granny mouse."

And this is precisely how the teenagers perform. As long as the round dance song goes on, everyone—the dancers and the audience—must frown and look angry. But the moment the song stops, the young people run out and point their fingers at an Elder and laugh. This is the only time in your whole life when you can make fun at an Elder—and the Elders love it most of all. As I indicated before, this is also a massive violation of proper conduct, where normally one would never "point" at anyone, let alone an Elder.

The result? The crowd erupts into laughter, and finds it impossible to keep an angry face. Just so, in this way, Ant Woman won once more. And this is one of the reasons this dance is done to formally end the powwow—it allows everyone to depart for their homes with laughter in their hearts and not a sense of anger over losing the contest.

In thinking up a recipe to go with this story, I thought about what sort of things Bear might eat in the story, but I decided a recipe for insect larvae wouldn't be a big hit for a lot of readers...

Remembering so many special people in my life who have crossed over—Bruce, Vi, my Aunt Beans and Aunt Prunie, I also thought about Roberta Wilson, a Lakota woman I met when I started graduate school. One Saturday in her kitchen, she showed me how to make what she called *Wojapi (also spelled Wojape)* in the Lakota language. It's a type of berry "pudding" that she would use on fry bread. It's a very simple recipe, but takes a bit of time to simmer down to intensify the flavor.

While traditionally it can be made with dried fruit—like dried chokecherries, because of Roberta, I've always associated it with freshly picked berries. I prefer huckleberries, but I also make it with blueberries. You can experiment with what you have available. Nowadays with many frozen berry choices so easy to find at your local grocery store, you can discover what you enjoy the most.

One of the realities of being shown how to do something is that there really aren't measurements, since amounts will vary according to how many berries you have, or how much *Wojapi* you want to make. Because there are no preservatives, I normally make *Wojapi* in small amounts, with the expectation it will be used up in a day or two. I've never tried freezing it.

Basically, the recipe consists of taking the amount of berries you want to use—a few handfuls of berries are what I will usually throw into a bowl. I'll mash them up with a potato masher, but I try to keep the mixture chunky, so I don't do it too thoroughly.

Some *Wojapi* makers prefer theirs to be smoother. I cover up the berries with water in a small sauce pan and start to simmer the mixture. If the berries are sweet enough, I don't feel a need to add sweetener to them. Others may add honey or sugar to taste.

Reducing the mixture down can be enough, but Roberta preferred to use flour to thicken it. Personally, I tend to use arrowroot or cornstarch for thickening. If you do too, make sure you mix the thickening agent separately into cold water and then when it's smooth, add it to the simmering berry mixture.

If you add it in directly, it's hard to keep lumps out. For the small amount I make, I will rarely use more than a teaspoon of thickening agent. If it's still not the consistency I want, I'll add in a little more of the arrowroot or cornstarch. If you put in too much, you can add additional water to thin it, until you finally get the balance you're wanting.

When I get it to the "Goldilocks Zone" of "just right," then I'll take it off the stove and let it cool, although depending on who was watching me make it, it might not have much of a chance to cool before it was being spread on fry bread, or whatever carbs were at hand. It also makes an excellent topping for ice cream. I'm sure Bear would approve.

The Girl Who Was Aiyaiyesh

Long and long ago there was a young girl that people would call Aiyaiyesh, which roughly would translate into English as "stupid." Even today, if you don't listen to your elders, people will say, "Ah, you're so aiyaiyesh."

Actually, in her later years, when she could no longer do beadwork because of arthritis, my grandmother would call her hands "aiyaiyesh," so a better translation into English would probably be "That which does not behave in an appropriate manner." But if you asked anyone at random on the reservation what "aiyaiyesh" means, they'd say "it means "stupid."

Other kids her age would help their Elders pick berries.

But not the girl who was aiyaiyesh…she would just sit underneath the cedar tree, watching the world go by.

Other kids her age would help their elders tan deer hides.

But not the girl who was aiyaiyesh—she would just sit underneath the cedar tree, watching the world go by.

Other kids her age would help their elders dig roots. But not the girl who was aiyaiyesh…she would just sit underneath the cedar tree, watching the world go by.

Other kids her age would gather cedar bark on the hottest days of the year to help their Elders. But not the girl who was aiyaiyesh—she would just sit underneath the cedar tree, watching the world go by.

Finally, one day, the cedar tree couldn't take it anymore and said, "Ah, you are so aiyaiyesh. All you ever do is sit underneath me. Now you watch. I'm going to show you how to do something."

And so it was the cedar tree showed her how to take the strong roots of the cedar and coil them around, sewing them together into a circle. Now circles are very sacred to most Native people. We're taught that the world is a circle—when the wind moves in its strongest power, it moves in a circle. In our ceremonies, when we pray, we turn in a circle because we are taught when you turn in a circle, one of your sins falls off.

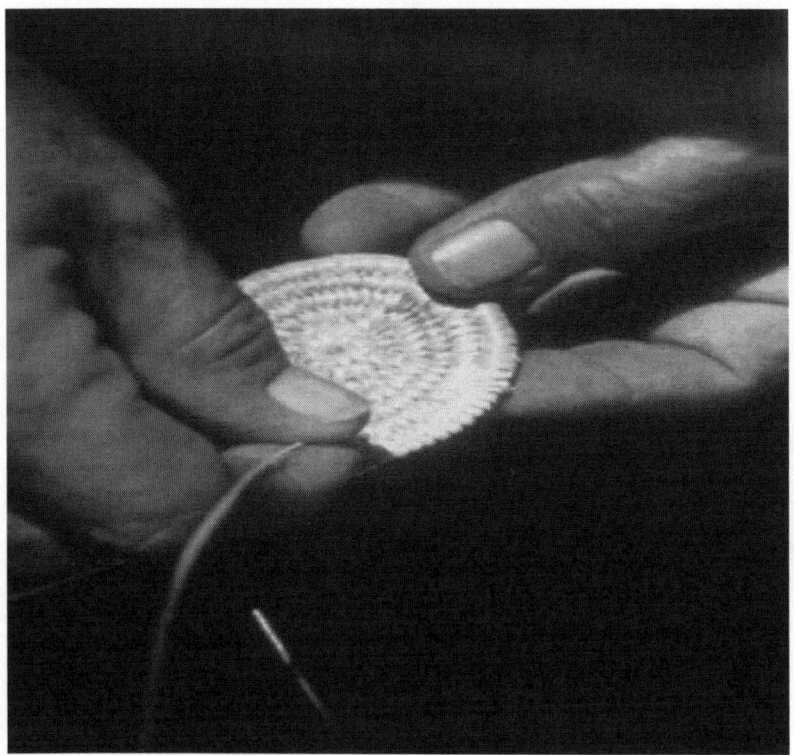

As she sewed the circles together, she created the very first hard root cedar basket. This is a very important thing in the Pacific Northwest. Not only is it traditionally used to contain berries, and other foods, but the baskets were so well made, they would hold water.

In fact one proof of moving into adulthood was to make four baskets which would then as a test, be dipped into water. If they would hold the water, then the basket maker was recognized as an adult. The baskets would then be given away to train the young person to always be generous. This type of basket was also used for cooking.

After being filled with water, small rocks that had been heated in a fire would be dropped into the water of the basket. The heat of the rocks would make the water boil, and you could then cook soups and stews.

But you had to be very careful and keep stirring the hot rocks around or they would stay at in one place and burn a hole through the bottom of your basket and you'd feel really aiyaiyesh.

When she had finished, the cedar tree examined her basket and told her she had done a good job, but she had woven no patterns onto her basket, and a basket was not finished until it had designs.

"But I don't know any designs," she cried.

"Ah, you're so aiyaiyesh," said the cedar tree. "Start walking—keep your eyes and your ears and your heart open, and you will find all sorts of patterns."

Just so, the girl began to walk and all along the way she was crying. In fact, she was crying so hard, she wasn't watching where she was going, and almost stepped on Waxpush, the rattlesnake. "What's the matter with you, almost stepping on innocent people!" the rattlesnake hissed.

"Oh, I'm so sorry," she answered, "but the cedar tree told me if I just kept walking, I'd find all sorts of designs for my basket, but I haven't found a single one."

"Ah, you're so aiyaiyesh," cried the rattlesnake. "Open up your eyes and see—just look at me!

And sure enough, when she looked—really looked at the rattlesnake, she saw she had a beautiful pattern of diamonds down her shiny back. "Oh, how beautiful you are! What a wonderful pattern!"

"Take it," said the rattlesnake, "use it for your basket." And so it was she wove the diamond back patterns into her basket.

When she was done, she was very proud of herself, but eventually she thought, "Well, I can't just keep using the same pattern over and over again," and she began to cry once more.

"Why are you crying, little girl?" called someone with a voice like thunder. She looked up from her tears and saw Patu, the Mountain, was talking to her.

"Oh, I'm crying because the cedar tree told me if I just kept walking, I would find all sorts of patterns for my baskets, but all I've found is just one!"

"Ah, you're so aiyaiyesh," called the Mountain. "You look at me—what do you see?" And sure enough, when she looked—really looked at the Mountain she saw that he was really a triangle.

"Oh, what a beautiful pattern you are," she said.

"Take it—and use it for your basket."

And so it was she wove the pattern of the Mountain into her basket.

She was very proud of herself, and as she kept walking, keeping her eyes and ears, and heart open, she saw all sorts of designs.

She saw lightning flash across the sky, and that gave her a new design.

The stars came out at night and formed constellations that she used for designs.

Butterflies danced around the flowers and taught her more patterns.

She saw how the leaves of the plants danced with the wind and her heart danced when she realized she had yet another design.

She saw the tracks of little birds. She saw the gills and the backbones of the Salmon and she wove these images into her baskets.

She saw the top knot on the little quail and that gave her a design she could use.

Everywhere she went, in every direction, she found patterns and designs.

And when she learned to weave all these designs into her baskets, she returned home to her people and taught them how to put the patterns into baskets.

When she had done that, she wasn't aiyaiyesh anymore.
(A traditional Sahaptin story, retold by Ty Nolan)

This is one of my favorite stories, and I have used it in getting across the idea of "Learning to See/Seeing to Learn." As a therapist, I find a lot of people are like the *aiyaiyesh* girl in the beginning of her journey—they keep using the same pattern (of behavior) over and over again. Part of their psychological growth comes from discovering that there are all sorts of other patterns (of behavior) around them that they can also use.

After I tell the legend, the first thing I will ask an audience is, "When did she stop being so *aiyaiyesh*?"

Was it when she learned to make a basket? Was it when she learned how to weave a design into the basket? Was it when she learned to see that patterns and designs were always all around her?

The legend says very specifically she stopped being *aiyaiyesh* when she was able to share her knowledge with her community. The beginning of the story states she is *aiyaiyesh*, and gives examples of what others her age would be doing during the four seasons (a cycle) of the year, in giving back to their community. But the girl doesn't give anything back. She only sits underneath the cedar tree and watches the world go by. Her *aiyaiyesh*-ness isn't about ignorance, but about her interactions and responsibility.

The knowledge of how to make the baskets described in the story was in danger of being lost not long ago. When I used to interview Native Elders for our TV program, **Native Vision**, I would hear them talk about how hard it was to make the baskets.

They involved almost a year of preparation—going out during the hottest days of the year to gather cedar bark when the sap would not be next to the surface where it would render the bark useless for basket-making—going into the higher elevations of the mountains to gather bear grass to weave into the basket—preparing alder bark to use as a reddish dye.

When the Native people would take their beautiful baskets into the White towns to trade, the settlers would dismiss them and offer used clothing for trade. I remember Hazel Pete, a respected Chehalis woman who came from generations of basket-makers, explaining to me how her mother told her as a child, "You are better than this. You are better than used and dirty old clothes."

Many stopped making the baskets, and started using buckets and pots obtained from their non-Native neighbors. Towards the last part of the 20th century, there was a revival of basket-making among many Native communities, and basket-making was even being taught in community centers on reservations.

On a spiritual level, this story is related to the Vision Quest, which involves discovering one's Power. In this case, the young woman would be about at the age of puberty, and her Spirit Power would be the Cedar Tree, which is responsible for helping her become all she can be. As my old friend, Joseph Campbell used to say, part of the Hero's Journey involves not only in leaving one's community in self-discovery—but also returning to the community to share one's vision.

In terms of the recipe I would like to pair with this story, I'm going to start with the assumption you either don't have a basket that you can use for cooking or if you do, it's likely to be a family heirloom you probably won't use for cooking anyway.

Because the NW traditions focus on soups and stews in the baskets, I decided to do a "Three Sisters Soup." I was aware of the Three Sisters (Corn, Bean, Squash) from southwestern culture and was pleased to find out much later as an adult that the Three Sisters are also very much part of other Native cultures, including up in the American Northeast, the homeland of the Six Nations Confederacy.

The legends say these are our relatives. On a practical level, the corn stalk forms a support for the beans to climb, while the beans attach nitrogen to the soil in a way that benefits the corn. The squash spreads out, helping keep the ground moist, but also discourages other plants (think about what most Americans would call weeds) and the spiny bits of the squash discourage a lot of pests.

If I'm in a hurry, (and it's one of those weeks) it's easy to throw together a can of black beans , a can of hominy, and a few cut up zucchini and yellow squash into a chicken stock (although I've been trying to be as productive as possible lately, so I've been freezing pork stock which I'll use instead). There's sometimes a mention of the Fourth Sibling—the spicy brother Chili, so I'll toss in enough crushed or ground red chili pepper until I'm satisfied.

I personally prefer cutting fresh corn off the cob to use, although sometimes I get a craving for hominy.

Depending on who will be sharing dinner, I might cut the fresh corn into segments for those who enjoy the experience of gnawing the corn off.

This is actually more representative of the Algonquian folks back east. *First appearing in English about 1778, "succotash" comes from an American Indian word for beans and maize cooked together. "Msiquatash" was the staple dish of the Narragansett tribe, who lived in what is now Rhode Island. A related Narragansett word, "asquutasquash," gave us "squash..."(Incidentally, the verb "squash," meaning "to smash flat," comes from an entirely different source, the Latin word for "break."*)

I'll also throw in a few diced tomatoes and garlic, and salt and pepper to taste. And because it's been a very busy week, I'll throw in the meat from the leftover pork that's been waiting patiently in the fridge. I'm ready to serve within 30 minutes, which includes tossing some rolls in the oven.

Chapter Four

How Butterflies Came To Be

Long and long ago, when the world was still new, the Creator watched children playing. He watched their sheer joy, and enjoyed their laughter. In the four directions he looked, he saw beauty—before him, behind, him, above him, and below him. He smelled the sweetness of flowers, heard the song of birds, saw the bright blue of the sky, and tasted the first touch of the coming cold on his tongue. This reminded him that time was passing—that winter would come again—that these children would all grow old and pass away as he had watched human children do over and over again. The leaves would turn brown and fall from the trees, and the flowers would fade to replenish the Earth.

He decided to create something to memorize this moment, something that would be a part of all this beauty. And so he gathered the blackness from the hair of the children's parents. He took the orange and reds of the falling leaves. He grabbed bits of sunlight, and the colors of the flowers. He took the evergreen needles of the pines. He took the soft whiteness of the clouds, and added all these things into a bag of buckskin. He smiled and after a moment, added the songs of the birds to his bag.

When he finished, he held the bag close to his heart, and called the children to him. He handed them his bag and told them to see what was inside. When they opened the bag, a cloud of butterflies emerged. They were like winged jewels. They were all the colors of the rainbow.

It was as if flowers were flying. The spirits of the children and the adults soared like hawks, for they had never seen anything like this before. The butterflies, light as a lizard's lick, touched on the heads and shoulders of their grateful audience. The butterflies swirled around and began to sing.

But then a bird flew to the Creator's shoulder and began to complain. "Why have you given our precious songs to these small and pretty beings? You have already made their wings more beautiful than ours—why give them our songs as well? You promised us that each bird would have his or her own song. It is not right to do what you have done."

The Creator looked at the small bird and nodded. "You are right. I promised one song for each bird, and it is not fair to give them away to others." So the Creator made the butterflies silent, and thus they remain today. But their beauty touches all people and opens up the songs in our own hearts.

Further south, it is said the world is a reflection of itself—the world of dreams and the world of work. It is taught these two worlds are like the wings of the butterfly. The dream world is one wing, and the working world is the other. The wings must connect at the heart for the butterfly to fly and live. Real life – true life—happens because of the movement of the wings. And this is what marriage is like. It mirrors the butterfly's heart, kept alive by the love of the husband and wife, moving together like twin wings.

(A traditional Tohono O'odham story (with a Mayan coda) retold by Ty Nolan)

I was asked by a friend, Paulette Friday, for help in finding an appropriate story for her to tell at a friend's upcoming wedding. I requested more details about those involved, and was told this was a couple in their 50's, and it was neither's first wedding. I suggested the butterfly story, for a number of reasons.

First, I wanted a story that wasn't overly long, since the focus should be on the ceremony and celebration rather than on a performance. I wanted a story that acknowledged a couple who are able to appreciate their experience of marrying again in a way a couple in their early 20s who have never been married can't fully imagine. That's why I emphasized in the story how the Creator both celebrated the moment of joy, but also had sadness that this was the autumn of life, rather than the spring.

Here's part of the e-mail I sent to her:

I thought this might be appropriate for your needs. I decided to do a retelling of a traditional Tohono O'odham legend. These are the people who are Native to the general Phoenix area, so it will let you bring a gift from where you have been. I then finished with a teaching from Native people further south—the Mayan.

In similar situations, after I would tell a story of this nature, I would then end by giving a small butterfly image as a gift to the new couple. I would probably then add the suggestion: "And in the weeks to come, you will see an image of a butterfly. Perhaps you will be at work, or perhaps you will be with the one you love. You will see a butterfly and you will smile, remembering this precious day."

She responded that she felt the story was "perfect for this couple," and that she would let me know how the event went.

One of the advantages of being from the southwest is the abundance of Zuni "fetish" carvings of various animals one can find at local Native Art shops. I notice that for butterfly "fetishes" the artists often use mother of pearl or abalone shells as their media, which I suspect, is to capture the iridescence of their models.

I was happy to find this in my e-mail a few days later–

Many, many thanks for sharing your version of the story of butterfly. I told this (with appropriate recognitions) at M's wedding last Friday. It was the perfect story for that perfect day. M and T and their family and friends loved it – it was especially significant to M (which was my intent). I followed your advice and gave them a butterfly fetish (Zuni) at the end of the story – the perfect touch!
–Paulette Friday

After I finished **Coyote Still Going**, I let Paulette know that I had included part of our email exchange, and had asked if she would feel comfortable if I shared her name as well. This was her response: *Your book is on my Kindle and I am already enjoying it. I recall your kind permission to use your Story of Butterfly at my friend's wedding - it was such a special gift. I continue to use that story with groups of elderly women in nursing homes who also love it and show appreciation with oohs and ahhs - and sometimes hugs. Your gift endures ;-)*

Why You Shouldn't Whistle At Night

She is tall... bigger than Sasquatch, and her body is covered with long, black, greasy hair. Her eyes are large like an owl's, and her fingers are tipped with sharp claws. Her lips are formed in the eternal pucker of an eerie whistle, and children are told if they don't listen to their Elders, she will come to them at night and suck their brains out of their ears. She is called At'at'lia, Dash-Kayah, Tsonoqua, and names whispered when the time is right, and not for publication.

Children are warned not to take food that she offers. If she catches you, she'll throw you inside the basket she carries on her back. Her basket is so large she can fit 10 children in it...and that's her favorite meal—10 children. She is a cannibal—she eats human flesh.

Long Time Ago—there was a young boy, named after the Silver Salmon. He woke up early in the morning and the warmth of the rising sun felt good on his face. He sang a song to thank the sun. The boy went out to go fishing but he went so far he realized he wouldn't be able to return home before the sun went down, so he decided to camp where he was.

It was late at night and the moon was full. Now White people tell us there's a man in the moon, but our Old People tell us it's really a frog. And so it was, the frog in the moon was looking down at him when clouds covered the moon and everything was dark.

Suddenly he heard a strange whistling, and the clouds blew away from the moon and he could see a monster standing in the darkness.

"Don't be afraid," she called out to him—"People make up terrible stories about me, but I'm really a very nice person. In fact," she said, holding out her hand, "I'm a very nice person. I have some berries for you—I know you must be hungry. Children are always hungry." And in her claw like hand he saw a pile of berries.

When he reached to take some of the berries, she took her other hand from behind her back. It was smeared with sticky sap from the trees. She slapped him with her hand and his eyes were glued shut! He was blind! She grabbed him up and stuffed him into her basket and ran through the woods whistling.

She came to a clearing and dumped him on to the ground. She had built a large fire and all around the fire were other children she had stolen. She was going to barbeque them.

She was so proud of herself, that she was going to have such a fine meal of young children, she started to sing and dance around the fire.

The boy was afraid, because he knew he would be eaten. He wished he could start his day over again. He thought of how his day had begun, with the warmth of the sun on his face. The warmth of the fire reminded him of the warmth of the sun. Just so, he leaned closer to the fire. The heat of the fire began to melt the sticky stuff on his eyes, and he could see again. As the Cannibal Woman continued to dance, he got an idea and whispered this idea to the girl next to him, who whispered it to the boy next to her—and so it went around the circle of the children.

When she finished, the monster was so tired she could hardly stand up—and that's when the boy shouted, "NOW!" And all the children jumped up and pushed her into the fire. She began to burn—but she didn't burn like ordinary things burn.

She burned like fireworks! Her body burst into a cloud of sparks—and that's where mosquitoes come from. They still live off the blood of young children, even today.

That was the end of Dash-Kayah—but she had three sisters—and those sisters are still around. And that's why we teach our children: "You must never whistle at night—because you don't want to call those spirit beings to you!"

(A traditional Twana story retold by Ty Nolan)

Something I always find interesting is how Stories will often vary from one community to another. After I left my position as Area Director of Head Start Programs on American Indian Reservations in Alaska, Washington, Oregon, Nevada, and Utah, I joined the staff of the National Bilingual Training and Resource Center. My Primary duty was to provide training and technical assistance to school districts in Alaska. My Secondary responsibility was to provide resources to school districts in Region 10 (Washington, Oregon, Idaho, and Alaska). Finally, my Tertiary duty was to work with American Indian bilingual programs nationally.

Because of my experience with "bush" (extremely rural) Alaska, I presented at a Bilingual Conference and was "discovered" by the

Government of the Northwest Territories in northern Canada. It made a lot of sense, because the languages I was working with in Alaska were similar dialects to those of the First Nations People in "the Great White North." I spent a number of years working with reserves with small communities and populations all across Canada.

In these communities (and those in bush Alaska), there usually wasn't a hotel. Normally non-Native consultants would end up in a sleeping bag in the high school gymnasium, because often the school was the only building in the village with electricity and running water. But because I was also Native, I would always be invited to stay in the homes of local people. Once I was in one of the most northern areas of Saskatchewan. The community entertained itself by playing bingo over the radio, since there was no television. I overheard the Elder who was hosting me tell her daughter I was from Alberta. That puzzled me until I discovered for her, Alberta was the furthest place she could think of.

That happened once with my mom, where one of my sisters asked me how I liked Bermuda. I had never been. When I asked my mom why she was telling people I had been in Bermuda, she was like the Saskatchewan Elder—"I just knew you were really far away, and the furthest place I could think of was Bermuda." As I traveled from Native community to Native community, the community people and I would usually share Storytelling. It would often feel as if there was one Story that had traveled as well, taking on slightly different shapes or flavors as it moved further west, or further east.

For example, I mentioned the Twana Story of Ant and Bear (or Why Ant Has A Small Waist) has a different twist among the Sahaptin, where Ant Woman's relatives danced with her. The Story of the Monster who stole young children to eat is told like this along the Columbia River:

Coyote and the Blood Monster

Long time ago, Coyote was going there. He was sought out by some of the Animal People because they were being attacked by Wawa-yai, a terrible Blood Monster. He was quite large and he had a nose that was as long and as sharp as a spear. This is how he would kill people—he would stab them with his nose and then drain their blood. He was too powerful for the Animal People to defeat, so they had set out to ask Coyote for his help.

There are many Stories that tell of Coyote's greed or his lack of responsibility, but there are many others that speak of Coyote's wit and bravery. He listened to them and told them he would help, but they would also need the assistance of the Plant People. Just so, Coyote went to the plants that had sharp thorns and asked if they would help the People. They agreed to do so.

Coyote organized the Animal People, with some of them lining the doors of the Longhouse with the Plants. Coyote supervised others in the making of Blood Soup. This was a traditional food, and it was prepared in the baskets. When the feast was complete, Coyote left and tracked Wawa-yai. He was very tall and skinny and frightening looking. Of course, he knew of Coyote. Everyone did.

"I come to invite you to a Feast," Coyote called out to him. "We will be serving wonderful and delicious Blood Soup. All you can eat."

Wawa-yai grew excited at the thought of Blood Soup and followed Coyote back to the Longhouse. "Why are all those plants around the door?" he asked Coyote.

"Aren't they beautiful? And they smell so nice—but don't stand around staring—hurry inside because the Blood Soup is waiting for you." Wawa-yai sat down and the Animal People began to bring out basket after basket of the Blood Soup they had prepared. Wawa-yai would stick his long nose into the basket and use it like a straw to drink every drop from the basket.

When he had walked through the door of the Longhouse, he was very skinny. But after a few baskets of Blood Soup, his belly began to grow. Coyote smiled and told the Animal People to keep bringing out more baskets of the Blood Soup. Wawa-yai kept sucking the baskets dry in his greed and gluttony. Soon his growing belly was hanging over his loincloth. His face was filling out with a double chin, and then a triple one.

"Isn't it delicious?" Coyote asked, offering yet another basket full of Blood Soup. Wawa-yai didn't answer because he was too busy emptying basket after basket of the Soup. The Animal People were exhausted from all their hard work. Now Wawa-yai was enormously fat with a huge round belly. He looked naked because his gut completely covered his loincloth.

"You've killed too many People," Coyote told him, and all the friendliness was gone from his voice. He was only a fraction of the size of the Blood Monster, but he stood up to him and said, "And I'm going to stop you from killing anyone else."

Wawa-yai struggled to stand up, his great belly almost pinning him down. He reached for Coyote, but the Monster was slowed down by his new size and weight. Coyote easily moved away and let Wawa-yai chase him. He was now so heavy that every footstep he took made the Longhouse shake. "You'll never catch me," Coyote laughed. "You're too fat and slow!" The Blood Monster was crazy with his anger and swore Coyote would be the next one to die.

Coyote continued to laugh and ran through the doorway. But now Wawa-yai was so fat, he was too wide to fit through the opening. As he tried to run through it, his bloated body hit the sharp thorns that surrounded the exit. When that happened, he exploded like a balloon being popped. *Wawa-yai* burst into tiny pieces. These became known as mosquitoes. They can no longer kill you, but they sure can make you itch!

(A traditional Sahaptin story retold by Ty Nolan)

Wawa is one of the words for mosquito. The *-yai* suffix throws it into what some Elders call "Legend Language," so you know an "everyday" mosquito is not being talked about.

One of the things I find different about a lot of Native American traditional Stories is they often don't end the way many older European tales do. In European culture, evil is usually identified and destroyed. There is always a dragon to slay. In versions of the Grimm stories, the Evil Queen or the Wicked Stepmother is forced to dance in red hot iron shoes until she dies. There seems to be an obligation to destroy what is perceived as evil (or often, simply as "different.")

But the Story of the Basket Monster who is pushed into the fire or the exploding Blood Monster doesn't end in their deaths, but in their transformations. For a number of Native languages, things are often conceptualized not as "good" or "bad"—"right" or "wrong." Rather a better translation would be "appropriate" or "inappropriate." "Useful" or "non-Useful."

I first worked with Barre Toelken through the Indian Readers Series I mentioned earlier. Barre has always identified himself as a "folklorist" so no one would mistake him for an anthropologist. For awhile he was married to a Navajo woman and lived on her reservation. He shared a story that one day a Navajo man came to his home and explained his wife was about to give birth, and they didn't have enough food. He had come to see if Barre would share with him.

Barre, being Barre, readily agreed, but added, "I happen to know you're a good hunter. It's deer season. If your family is going hungry, why don't you just get a deer?" The man did not immediately answer Barre. He finally said, "Because it is not appropriate that I who am about to receive life, should be taking life at this time." For a lot of Native peoples, there's the concept that it isn't just the expectant mother who is pregnant—the expectant father is as well. That means there are certain ritual responsibilities he has, just as the mother to be has. Just so, it's about context, where hunting a deer is not "right" or "wrong," but in the context of the pregnancy, it would be "inappropriate."

Just so, beings like the Wawa-yai, or Dash-Kayah are perhaps better understood not to be monsters per se, but they are "out of balance." They are no longer living in Harmony, and that brings disorder to the world around them. They are not so much defeated as they are transformed. Transformation is almost always a major theme in Native spirituality and culture.

In the Pacific Northwest, there is a very special type of carved wooden mask called a Transformation Mask. The outer Mask of the Monster Woman shows her frightening aspect. But at one point in the ceremony, hidden strings are pulled, and the Mask splits open, revealing a human face within.

Like the Story of Abalone Girl and Gold Girl, these legends remind us to always be aware there will be more than one level of reality. Dash-Kayah, or Tsonoqua, is a very common image used in totems, on tool handles, on drums or as Feast bowls.

An old friend of mine, Joseph Campbell has talked about the role of frightening figures like the Tsonoqua to scare off the uninitiated—the ones who are not yet ready to enter into the

Sacred Place. In this way they serve the purpose of Guardian figures placed in front of the Longhouses. But they welcome those who understand what is truly beneath the surface.

I have also used the Dash-Kayah story in both doing therapy with people who had substance abuse problems and in substance abuse prevention. If you've ever worked with someone who has an addiction, it can feel like a huge and all-powerful monster. A person can feel as small and powerless as a young child. But the legends tell you if you behave in an appropriate way—your troubles don't disappear (which is one of the problems in using a traditional European tale, where the story really does end with the defeat/eradication of a challenge). But your troubles can become manageable. Dash-Kayah or the Wawa-yai don't suddenly vanish—but they can become something you can live with on a daily basis.

I mentioned much of this book first appeared on a blog I was doing, and I received some very negative feedback on a post I had done about our beloved dog, who had gotten into trouble (as in being able to locate and scarf down decaying bird carcasses). My most profound apologies to those I offended by that post: "Why Dog Does Stupid Things," who felt I did not respect the nobility of Dog. In fact, it was suggested by a reader American Indians did not appreciate dogs to the extent non-Natives do.

I think it would be better understood that the story I had shared on the blog was reflective of how some American Indians try to make sense of why, when Dog, who normally is so loving and caring—well, sometimes does stupid things. When an Elder laughingly says, "Oh, why did you have to choose *Dukwaps*," it's an expression of affection. There's never a question about the love one has for Dog. No matter what Dog does—you still love Dog.

There's a Twana word that has no direct translation into English. *Dukwaps*. Elders say it means "Something so stupid, only a dog would do it."

Why Dog does Stupid Things

Long and long ago, The Creator was giving out gifts to all the Animal People.

To Eagle, The Creator gave powerful eyes to see.

To Bear, The Creator gave the ability to heal.

To Beaver, The Creator gave the skill of working with wood.

To Wolf, The Creator gave great hunting prowess.

At last, when the bag of gifts was almost empty, The Creator looked inside and saw there was only one item left...Dukwaps.

"Who wants Dukwaps?" called The Creator.

Dog (Who had already been given Faithfulness) yelled back, "—I'll take it!"

And so it is, even today, when a dog does something so stupid, only a dog would do it, Elders say, "Why did you have to choose Dukwaps?"

(A traditional Twana story retold by Ty Nolan)

One of the suggestions was that I share an additional legend that's also part of our tradition—that explains why there is so much fondness as well as respect for Dog. I should also mention that some of the coastal traditions report a nobility connection with Dog. A High-Class woman had a secret lover who would only come to her at night. When she shared with her closest friends she wondered who he was, they suggested she cover her hands with red ochre (paint) and smear his back when she next had relations with him. They told her, "Look at the back of those you see in the village the next day." To her surprise, the next day, she saw Dog with smears of red paint on his back.

Now, depending on which Native Nation's legend you know, when her father, the Chief, found out she had been intimate with Dog, some say Dog was killed (others say Dog later took on a human shape and went with her), and she was set adrift in a canoe. Some say her brother went after her to protect her. When she gave birth, her babies were puppies. She and her brother watched over them. But when her brother went hunting to provide for them, she discovered the puppy children would wait until they weren't watched, and they would take off their puppy skins and turn into human shaped children. Eventually, the mother and brother hid and when the children took off their puppy "robes," the brother ran out and gathered their puppy skins and threw them into the fire.

Some say one of the puppy children was able to snatch his skin out of the fire and remained in that form. The destruction of their puppy skins forced them to retain their human shape. Various Native (American and Canadian) Nations trace their lineage from these children. Of interest to *Twilight-New Moon* novel/movie fans, at least as many Native Nations claim their heritage is from the Wolf.

Why Dog (and Horse) Is So Special

Long and long ago, Human Beings were created after the Animal People. The Creator called the Animal People together and asked them to help the new Humans. "They are weak and soft. They will not be able to survive without your help." The Creator asked the Animal People to instruct the Human People how to gather and prepare food, the way Wolf and Bear and the others did so well. The Creator asked others to teach them how to run and move; how to do weavings and how to build things with the skill of Beaver and others.

To the surprise of the Animal People, the Human Beings not only learned quickly, but adapted these teachings to their own advantage.

The Animal People gathered together. Many called out: "Human Beings will soon surpass us with the knowledge we have so generously provided them. Soon they will overtake us and treat us badly. We must kill them now so they do not dominate us!"

Only Dog and Horse argued on behalf of the Human Beings. They asked the other Animal People not to kill them. But the Animal People fought with one another, and Dog and Horse realized they could not win. With great bravery—knowing the other Animal People might indeed kill them as traitors—Dog and Horse went to the Human village and warned them of the danger. The Human beings fled and hid.

When the Animal People attacked the Human village, they found The Creator waiting for them.

"I asked you to help the Human Beings, and you responded by choosing to kill them. To punish you, I will take away the power of

universal language from you. No longer will you be able to speak to one another as you have. Because Dog and Horse sought to protect the Human beings, I will let them retain their Power of Communication."

Just so, even now, Dog and Horse are able to "speak" with Human beings in a way no other Animal People can.

(A Sahaptin legend retold by Ty Nolan)

In the Sahaptin language, the name for Horse is "*kusi*" and the name for Dog is "*kusi kusi*." Depending on how you think of things, this means a dog is a small horse, or a horse is a large dog.

I was told by a Cherokee Elder Native people had horses before the Europeans arrived, but they were smaller and had longer fur than the European horses. There is clear archeological evidence this was so:

American Indians had dogs long before non-Natives arrived. Most of these Native dogs are "lost," having interbred with the newcomers non-Natives brought with them (just as it's been suggested the surviving Native Horses interbred with the newly arrived European horses). For example, Elders in the Pacific Northwest talk about small wooly dogs—their fur was used to weave blankets.

"Finally, there's the question of what makes people and dogs such inseparable friends. Using a number of behavioral experiments–most of them involving finding food hidden in scent-camouflaged boxes–a team headed by anthropologist Brian Hare of Harvard compared the ability of wolves, adult dogs and puppies to pick up subtle cues in human behavior. Both puppies and dogs showed a talent for finding the food using nonverbal signals from the researchers–even something as subtle as gazing toward the hiding place.

"That doesn't surprise Nicholas Dodman, director of the Animal Behavior Clinic at Tufts University School of Veterinary Medicine. Dodman says dogs can read 'a look, a facial expression, a tone in your muscles.' Wolves, by contrast, are dolts when it comes to reading such signs—suggesting that the trait arose during domestication."

Roots and Wings

Long and long ago, there was a great Chief. He had a son, and loved him very much. "One day," he always told others around him, "my son will not only grow up to be a Great Chief, but a powerful Medicine Man as well."

The boy heard this, but did not think anything of it.

When it was time, the boy was prepared for his Vision Quest. For a girl this is when she is usually first tied to the Moon, and for boys, it is often when their nipples turn out. Traditionally, the Vision Quest will take place on the top of a mountain, or by running water. A child is taken to the place of the Vision Quest, mentored by a Medicine Person. The Vision Quest helps a person discover who they are meant to be—a purpose and a reason for being.

"My son," called the Chief, "will become a powerful Medicine Man. For that reason, I summon seven Medicine Men from the four directions to watch over him—to prepare him for his Vision Quest." And so seven Medicine Men came, some from very far away.

In the traditional manner, they painted him with red ochre.

This is considered to be a type of protection. When someone is involved in spiritual things, he or she will shine, and it will attract the attention of things of the spirit. Some of these are indifferent, some are dangerous and some are kind. The red paint is to keep away those things that are not kind.

A Vision Quest will traditionally take 4 days and 4 nights. During this time, the Seekers will not eat. He or she will fast, and take only as much water as they can hold in their mouths at one time. The first day went by, and there was no vision. The second day—no vision. The third day—no vision.

On the fourth day, when nothing had happened, the Medicine Men returned to the boy's father. "Perhaps he is not yet ready," one said. "There is no shame in this. Different people grow in different ways. Let us bring him back and have him try again at a later time."

"No," the Chief replied. "You know, and I know that the longer it takes for a vision to occur, the more powerful it will be. That is why he has not received his vision. Paint him again!"

And so it was the Medicine Men returned to the boy, painting him again with more of the red paint. A fifth day went by without a vision. A sixth day. A seventh. The Medicine Men returned to the boy's father. "No one has ever fasted this long," said one.

"We fear this is not his time," said another. "We ask that you let us bring him back. Let him continue his Vision Quest at another time."

"No!" said the Chief. "You are all jealous because you know that he will not only one day be a Great Chief, but one day he will be more powerful than any of you! Paint him again, and let the Vision Quest continue!"

The Medicine Men returned to the boy. They repainted him with the red paint. Nine days went by without a vision. Then ten. Then eleven. On the twelfth day, the Chief went himself to the place of the Vision Quest. His son was gone.

Frightened, he ran through the woods, calling out his son's name. A small bird followed behind him. Finally, exhausted, he sat down on the stump of a tree, his eyes full of pain—for he truly loved his son.

The little bird approached him. "I was your son," the small bird said.

"All my life you would tell other people that I would one day be a Great Chief. That I would one day be a powerful Medicine Man. But never once did you ever ask me what I wanted. I did not desire to be a Chief. I did not desire to be a Medicine Man. I just wanted to be myself. The Creator took pity on me, and gave me this shape to wear.

It is to teach parents that they must not force their own dreams on their children. They must give their children roots and wings. They must help their children become who they are meant to be."

In English, we call that little bird the Robin. And so it is even today when you see a Robin it still wears the red paint from long ago.

(A traditional Sahaptin Legend retold by Ty Nolan)

In the Pacific Northwest, the red ochre (and other colors) is often mixed with elk marrow used as a base, so the paint can be easily applied. The elk marrow is also a salve that speeds up healing of the skin. For example, an Elder used it on me when I had developed some blisters from constant drumming while helping someone being initiated into Winter Spirit Dancing. It was amazing to me how quickly the blisters vanished.

The tradition for many Native Nations is to have the first Vision Quest take place around puberty, but there are certainly stories of younger children who did this. Over the years, when the American and Canadian governments attempted to suppress Native traditions, some people had to wait until later in life to be initiated or to go for a Vision Quest. For some people, a number of Vision Quests might take place during a lifetime. There are also many stories of people spontaneously receiving their visions/spirit songs after a tremendous personal tragedy or trauma. For example, this happened to a mother whose children had died when their home caught on fire, and during their funeral, she went into an altered state and began to sing her new spirit song.

The Origin of the Bear Clan

Long time ago, the daughter of a Chief was warned by her elders to be careful as she went to pick berries, because many bears were around. She went out anyway, and as she drew near the berry bushes, she stepped into bear dung.

Upset, she cursed the bears, as she tried to clean herself. Bear people emerged from the woods and abducted her. Inside their cave, she sat sadly in a corner, until a tiny thin voice spoke to her and she looked into the bright wise eyes of Grandmother Mouse.

"Tell them they must take you out to relieve yourself–and that as a proper person, you must do this in privacy." Then Grandmother Mouse touched the gleaming copper bracelets that the young woman wore, indicating her high-class status. "Take off your bracelets and break them into small pieces and leave them on the ground." Traditionally, copper was very valued by Native people—it is the one of the only metals that can be used directly from the ground without smelting.

When the young woman did as she was instructed, the Bear people inspected where she had gone to relieve herself and whispered to one another. "No wonder she complains of our dung. She is so high-class that her dung is pure copper!"

Impressed, they informed the Bear Chief, who married the young woman, and thus the Bear Clan began. Many Native artist have depicted the human mother breast feeding her cubs.

(A Traditional Twana legend, retold by Ty Nolan)

Let me close for now with one of my favorite Stories. On one level I don't think a Storyteller should have a favorite Story, any more than a parent should have a favorite child. But that happens as well.

Coyote's Eyes

Long time ago, Coyote was going there. He saw something very strange—something very mysterious. He saw a wîlaalik—*a rabbit. But this was no ordinary rabbit—this was a Twati—a medicine person. As Coyote watched, the Twati began to sing. Suddenly the eyes of the rabbit flew out of his head and landed above them on the branch of a tree. This amazed Coyote. Then the Twati yelled, "Weenum! (Come here!"). His eyes flew off the branch and settled like falling leaves, entering back into his eye sockets so he could see again.*

Coyote ran up to the rabbit and begged, "Show me that trick! I want to learn that trick!"

"Oh, no, Coyote," the Twati told him. "This is not for you." Coyote kept begging the Twati, and finally the rabbit agreed. "I will teach you how to do this thing, Coyote, but you must never do it more than four times in one day. If you do it more than four times in one day, something terrible will happen to you."

"No problem," Coyote said. "Just show me the trick!" When Coyote learned the Song, he sang it, and sure enough, his eyes flew out of his head and sat on the branch of the tree above him. Meanwhile rabbit left to go into another legend.

Proud of what he could now do, Coyote called his eyes back to him and they obediently returned and he could see again. He did this a second time, then a third time. He did it a fourth time and thought, "Why am I wasting my time doing this here where no one can admire how clever I am?" So Coyote set out for the closest village. He called all the people together and said, "Now, check his out!"

He sang the song, and sure enough, his eyes floated up and landed on the branch of a tree. Everyone around him was very impressed, just as you'd be impressed if my eyes fell out of my own head.

"That's nothing," laughed Coyote. "Now watch this!" He yelled "Weenum!"

And nothing happened. He yelled it again, and the eyes just sat there, looking down at everyone. Just then a crow flew by and thought, "Lunch!" and ate Coyote's eyes. The village people could take a joke, so they laughed and left Coyote alone. Coyote was very worried. He thought and he thought about what to do, but he couldn't think of anything. Finally, in desperation, he turned to his sisters for help

Now Coyote has three huckleberry sisters who live inside his stomach, and when he can't think of what to do, he'll ask them to assist him. He called on his sisters, and they jumped out of him and landed before him on the ground. "What is it this time, Coyote?" the first one asked.

"Always bothering us," said another. "Always asking us what you should do."

"And when we tell you what to do you always say, "Oh, that's what I was going to do anyway."

"We're sick and tired of this, Coyote," said the first one. "This time you can just figure it out for yourself. We aren't going to help you."

Coyote grew angry at his sisters. He began to sing a song of his own. The clouds above grew black and heavy looking. There was a flash of lightning and the roll of thunder because Coyote was calling forth hail. Now huckleberries hate hail because it hurts their little leaves and branches.

"No, no," yelled one, "Call off your hail, Coyote."

"Yeah," said another—we know what it is you want to know anyway."

"You want to know what to do about your eyes," sighed her sister.

"Use flowers for your eyes," said the oldest one.

"Flowers?" Coyote repeated.

"Yeah, Flowers," said the youngest one. But in our language she meant a very specific type of flower that even today we literally call "Coyote's eyes." It looks a lot like a daisy.

"Oh," said Coyote. "I knew it all along. That's what I was going to do anyway!" His sisters were disgusted and jumped back inside of him. He quickly felt his way around and finally found some. He put them into his empty eye sockets—and he could suddenly see again. He was thrilled and he spent the rest of the day wandering around and looking at things. Everything went fine until the sun began to go down. Now this flower does something very special when the sun sets. It closes up.

Suddenly he was blind, and he realized his sisters had tricked the Trickster. He had to spend the whole night blind. The next morning when the sun came out, he had to feel his way around in his blindness until he found a fresh pair. Then he went to find someone he could trick. He had gone so far, it wasn't until late afternoon he saw anyone. It was a Native woman, who had a very large basket on her back, filled with berries she had been picking.

Coyote showed off his flower eyes. "Do you see how wonderful and magical my eyes are?" She looked at him and he said, "And I can see so many things." He leaned to his side, looking around the woman and into the distance. "Why I can even see what your husband is doing while you're working so hard over here."

"Gee," she said, "I'd sure like be able to see like that."

"You do?" Coyote smiled. "I'll tell you what—let's just make a straight trade. You give me your old ordinary everyday eyes and I'll give my magic flower eyes!"

"Will it hurt?" she asked.

"Nah," he said, "I won't feel a thing. Give me your eyes!" So they traded and now Coyote had normal eyes again and she had Flower eyes. She was looking around and just about then the sun started to go down and she went blind.

"You tricked me!" she yelled. "I don't want these old things! Give me my own eyes back."

Now Coyote grew angry with her and said, "If you don't want these eyes, then you'll have no eyes at all! You'll spend all eternity having to feel your way around the way I had to feel my way around." Then he used his Tamanawis (his Spirit Power) on her and she began to shrink. She became smaller and smaller until she became Shuckshya—the Snail. The big basket on her back became her shell. And even now when you see the Snail, she has to feel her way around the way Coyote did.

(A traditional Sahaptin story, retold by Ty Nolan)

As I've mentioned before, our Stories are often teaching us how to see in new ways. If we feel stuck, it's often because we're using an inappropriate set of eyes. Sometimes we need to borrow the eyes of the Eagle to see far and understand the "big picture" of things. Other times we need be borrow the eyes of Mouse and concentrate on how to immediately feed and support our family and loved ones.

It is common for Elders to present young people with beaded medallions.

One of the teachings that goes with the gifting of the medallion is to tell the young person, "You are the center of the medallion—you are the center of your own world." They are shown how the individual beads that surround the center make up the elaborate and beautiful patterns. If you are trying to look too closely, you don't see a pattern at all. You only see those beads (people, events, experiences) directly around you, and this means the pattern will be invisible to you. It can become too easy to believe there is no order or meaning to the world. As you back away, you being to see all these different colors (different people, different cultures, and different spiritual paths) really do come together—not only in a design, but in a beautiful one.

And it may well be the only one who can have the appropriate perspective is The Creator.

The Snail woman bought into the idea that someone else's way of seeing is inherently superior to her own, rather than understanding no one way of seeing is the best way—it all depends on what you need to see. She was willing to give up her sacred individuality in order to obtain a way of seeing she did not really understand, and so she lost the options of being able to truly see. This is one of the challenges in trying to pass on traditional teachings, language, and culture to our children. It has become so easy for them to use the eyes of others—from their schools, television, movies, and the Internet.

The Snail woman story is not about one way of seeing being better than another—it's about the importance of the diversity of perception. Like the Navajo hunter who would not kill a deer while his wife was pregnant—it's about discovering what the most appropriate—the most useful perception one can use in a specific situation.

I had mentioned my friend Barre Tolkein before. He shared a story about being on the doctoral committee for a Navajo graduate student. The student had not decided on a dissertation project, and was assigned one that had to do with a particular algae. It was unusual because it had the properties of more than one type of algae. Being able to use an electron microscope, the young man saw the algae appeared to be moving in more than one direction at the same time. He was able to easily express this in the Navajo language—but not in English. When he showed his advisors what he was seeing, they simply saw the same old algae.

But the Navajo language is structurally different than most Indo-European languages. There is an inherent sense of relationship built in. If I look out the window and see a car go by, that's exactly what I can say in English. But in Navajo, a speaker has to express whether or not the viewer is in motion, or is stationary. The car must be described as moving towards one or moving away. Is the car stationary, or is it in motion? The wonderful irony is—Navajo, the traditional language of a people who were often shepherds—is much more expressive in discussing technology than English.

Imagine a rocket shooting through the air. A scientific observer must be aware of the fact the rocket is not just moving—it is also rotating. It is also moving in the context of Earth, which is not only moving, but simultaneously revolving, while it circles the sun. Navajo is very good at expressing movement.

After much thought, the young man went to Barre, feeling he lacked the technical skills to show his advisors what he knew he was seeing. He explained as a child, he would watch the sheep being butchered. There was an invisible membrane around the muscle. He explained that he was taught to spit on the membrane and the enzymes in his saliva would start to dissolve the membrane so it could be peeled off and removed. "So," he concluded, "do you think it would be alright if I spit on my slide?"

Barre asked him if he had enough slides, where if this didn't work, his research would not be endangered. When the student assured Barre there were plenty of slides, Barre told him to go spit on his slides. When he did, the enzymes in his saliva dissolved the coating of the algae, and two organisms popped out. He had seen the algae moving in different directions at the same time because he was observing two organisms with a symbiotic relationship.

This was a young man who was able to use more than one set of eyes at the same time. He was able to switch back and forth to discover a more useful way of seeing. This is one of the reasons it is so vital that not just Native American—but all traditional cultures and understandings need to be preserved.

There is a Japanese story that describes an old man on a mountain top. Down below on the shore, his neighbors were amazed to discover the ocean had disappeared, and the water's floor was exposed. In wonder they walked in an area they had never seen before. But the old man knew what was happening. He knew this was a tsunami in progress—the water that was gone would soon come rushing back.

He could not yell loud enough to warn his neighbors, and he did not have the strength to run down and have them follow him back up the mountain. Just so, he set fire to his fields. His neighbors saw the smoke and ran to his aid-rushing up the mountain as the water returned. They were saved because they sought to save their Elder. The bottom line—we will never know what it is we need to save. We have no way of knowing which legend, which Story, which plant, or teaching we are going to need to face the challenges that are coming.

Our traditional Stories are often a type of map. They tell you where you have come from, where you are, and where you need to go. For example, HIV/AIDS may be a relatively "new" disease, but we have many traditional Stories that give us guidelines about how to face challenges (like Dash-Kayah, like Wawa-yai) that at first seem overwhelming, but can be dealt with if we behave in an appropriate way. As a therapist, and as an educator, I have seen people with Stories so powerful, these people don't tell their Story—their Stories tell them. Their Stories become a type of script they follow.

One of the things I have always tried to teach my students—the only difference between medicine and poison is the dosage. Some Stories have the Power to heal. But there are also Stories that can kill. These are the Stories that tell you that you are nothing—that you have no meaning—that you are unloved.

In the Stories of the American Southwest, Grandmother Spider is often mentioned. She is understood by some to be the Creatrix of the World. Isn't that a wonderful word in English? It means the female Creator. Her symbol is the web. Native people know from long observation it does not matter where you touch on a spider's web—a ripple goes throughout the whole.

I would suggest when there is pain-where there is trauma, for the individual, it can feel as if the individual threads that connect them the Web of Life have been severed—that there is no longer a sense of connection—a sense of belonging. In some of the versions of the European fairytale, Cinderella's stepsisters try to force their feet into her glass slipper. When they don't fit, they attempt to solve their problem in as direct a warrior way as the Deer legend—they begin to slice off the parts of themselves that don't fit something that was never made for them in the first place.

One cuts off her toes—the other cuts off her heel, and then they try to stuff their bloody stumps into what will never fit. I have watched many people—of all ages, of all ethnicities, of all religions, and different sexual orientations, attempt to be what they are not, because they have been taught a Story there is only one way to be—only one way to be accepted.

There is a Story that there is a thread that attaches our heart to the heart of the Creator. When we do something that brings us shame—that we feel is wrong—that thread breaks. In the process of healing the thread is tied back together. But the nature of knots is such, each time it happens, the thread is shortened. This means in the process of healing, the distance between your heart and the heart of the Creator is lessened, and you grow closer.

I have always loved to discover the meaning of words. When I used to do so much work in the field of HIV/AIDS, I would try to explain the difference between curing and healing. Curing means a cessation of the symptoms. Healing means a restoration of wholeness. In the early days of AIDS, before the current medications, it was not possible to cure someone of the disease. But with all diseases, there can be the possibility of healing, even if there is no chance of a cure. I have been honored to witness families that had been broken come back together because they realized the love they had for a family member was more important than the hatred and prejudice they had because of the individual's sexual orientation or drug addiction.

In these cases, the patient might die—but he or she did so in the process of a healing family. Years ago I remember watching a television program where the host was interviewing a physician who specialized in terminally ill children, several of whom were on the set. In a very insensitive way, the host asked the doctor in front of his young patients—"How can you stand to work with these children, knowing they're going to die?"

The physician responded: "We're all going to die. These children just have a better sense of when."

When I look at the Spider Woman's Web of Life, I am always aware the origin of the word "Heal" is the word "Whole," which is the root word for "Holy." It is the restoration of the Wholeness of Life and each individual—that contributes to the Healing—and the Holiness of us all. When the stepsisters cut off parts of their feet—in English we use the word "dismember." It meant to tear or cut apart. Do you know what the opposite of dismember is? It's the word "Remember." One of the powers of the Best Stories is helping you remember who you truly are.

<< >>

If you enjoyed my **Coyote Still Going: Native American Legends and Contemporary Stories**, please consider leaving a review where you purchased it, or on Goodreads. It would mean a great deal to me. Thank you.

Please visit my Amazon Author's page to learn of my upcoming work: amazon.com/author/tynolan

You might also want to check out my novel, **Memoir of A Reluctant Shaman (A Native American Story of Magical Realism)**. The first chapter was a finalist for National Public Radio's Short Fiction Contest under the title "Dolls" by Ty Nolan. Now read the full story of a most remarkable family.

Did you love *Coyote Still Going: Native American Legends and Contemporary Stories*? Then you should read *Memoir of a Reluctant Shaman (A Story of Native American Magical Realism)* by Ty Nolan!

From the NY Times and USA Today Best Selling Author Ty Nolan (Available for a limited time only at $.99)

"My grandmother's song would make her wooden dolls dance without strings, something I have sought to do in my own relationships without much success. Perhaps my song is not strong enough, or perhaps I would be better off with stiffer relationships than the blood and bone-based lovers I've chosen--or that have chosen me.

Living in cities that are so bright they blot out the stars at night, my lovers have had skin washed pale as fish bellies back home, and I have never quite figured out how to explain to them what happens on our reservation, where stars look new and are strong enough to burn our bodies brown.

How do I explain to my vegetarian significant other that he can buy a t-shirt in the tribal store that reads, "Vegetarian is an Indian word for poor hunter." How do those for whom meat is something wrapped in plastic you use plastic to buy, make sense of my siblings hacking meat off a still-warm carcass? Do they really understand that the smooth hardness of the drums of mine they touch and admire is the flesh of the animal scraped clean?"

Thus begins a coming of age story of Native American Magical Realism. The first chapter was a finalist in National Public Radio's Short Fiction Contest under "Dolls." Now discover the full story of a most remarkable family.

Printed in Great Britain
by Amazon.co.uk, Ltd.,
Marston Gate.